Lunelio's Epic Journey

Copyright© 2018 Luis Rodriguez & Alchemy Hero Publishing
Cover & Illustrations Copyright© 2018 Alchemy Hero Publishing
Library of Congress Cataloging-in-Publication Data

ISBN 978-0-9975433-7-7

Written by Luis Rodriguez
Illustrated by Leonardo Ariel Ariza Ardila
Illustration Assistant Marcus Hadlock
Edited by William Grabowski

To my children Iolani Lucia and Teyo Luis, my wife, my nephews Matisse, Miguelito, and Jackson, and the rest of my precious family, friends, and students present and past.

Preface

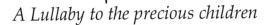

A Lullaby to the precious children

To the thing under my bed with eyes hungry and red.
So many nights the fear of my dreams dripped and bled.
Whirling confusion if the sounds were real or in my head.
"Is anyone there?"
Darkness's smirking silence filled me with dread.
"Oh yes. Oooh Yesss. And I'm done waiting, to be — FED!"

Glossary

Bro-migo, Compa, Bro-mano, Bro-slice, Bro-ski: terms that stand for my brothers from other mothers.

You will also find words, like Easter eggs, in Spanish. Feel free to ask a bilingual friend or Google them.

It Came for Me

I had just turned five and lay sleeping, blue cake-icing nearly fresh on my lips. A strange smell woke me. Sweat beaded my forehead in the room's sudden heat, and I swore I could hear breathing, heavy and patient, scratching the silence. I could hear and feel my heart thumping.

I could even hear, as the breathing quickened, that the sound huffed from under my bed. If there were anything in the world more frightening, I could not imagine it.

I clenched my teeth so hard my ears rang.

My abuelita had started teaching me magic, and my brain whirled searching for a spell. No dice. Fear froze me.

I tried to scream.

No luck—choked with terror, my throat only clicked and gulped. The bed shook suddenly as if from an earthquake. As if that weren't bad enough— *man!*—fiery red light bloomed beside it.

"Come here, boooyyy," rumbled a voice, guttural and—I *knew*—far from human.

And you know where it came from, right? Under my—A pitchfork of a hand whipped up and clamped my arm.

Now I did scream, 'cuz my flesh burned from— I could see—the grip of that hand, charred and flaking.

The room stank, and again I cried out.

My abuelita kicked through the door, and blasted some of her true magic. This unclenched the demon's "hand," and my parents yanked me out of the room.

* * *

Neither the police nor my parents believed a demon tried to take me that night, but my abuelita knew the truth.

In all the commotion and terror, my bedroom window got smashed. The cops, always "logical," insisted it had been done by some criminal — part of a child-smuggling operation. Right!

I knew what I saw and it couldn't be human!

The sinister thing generously left me with more than a handprint tattooed onto my arm.

After the cops left, my parents took me to the bathroom mirror. Moms tears endlessly poured. My *hair* . . .it had turned white. All of it. I mean like Santa-beard white!

In the beginning it seemed kinda cool, but not anymore. I looked like an old-man kid. My moms called me her little silver fox. I had to constantly remind her, "It's not silver, it's old man butt-hair white." A new home, therapy, becoming an expert at ignoring people, and an epic crew of friends helped me finally feel normal … ish. And *now* that bleeping thing came back. To make matters worse, a greasy gorilla-sized bully wanted to pounce the life out of me. O.M.G!

Too much drama. Would I survive? Hmm, probably not...

* * *

Did Someone Order a Coffin?

(3 days ago)

I walked into the lunchroom holding the most important dessert of my life. Normally, Math, one of my main bro-mano, would be waiting for me. Everyone called him Math because he, like a whiz, he turned mistakes with words, numbers, and science formulas into crunchy success sandwiches.

Where could he be? Moths enjoyed their trampoline party in my belly.

Why?

Because of a girl. Her name — Viorica, aka my crush.

And I had a date with her *today*. Well … not a date, but she did ask me to sit with her during lunch. Why? I had *no* idea. The *why* didn't matter. I just felt happy she remembered I existed.

Faking a poker-face, I stepped into the cafeteria. Hairnetted lunch ladies plopped lumpy gray slop on kids' trays. I swear that gunk, typical of any public school, squirmed on the yellow trays. Near the seating area, I scanned for Viorica — and hoped not to look like a goggle-eyed creeper.

There! *Yikes*. Stealthily, cradling boxed raspberry chocolate pie, I approached. A sudden foul stench tainted the air — my stomach soured.

A shadow broke over me, stained the floor. My ears popped. Gruff breathing heated the back of my neck, and I knew the sinister beast had returned.

"HUR HUR HUR."

The grotesque sound rattled my ears and I slipped.

Oh bleep — my epic dessert! Struggling not to fall, I watched my feet rehearse a drunken moon-walk through grease. Don't try this at home — or *any*where.

All those hours with my dance crew kicked in and I caught my balance.

Before I could turn around a giant force launched me into empty air with no parachute. Me, my cotton-white hair, and a delicious pie flew. Sometimes life seemed *so* unfair. I had gone through so much to make this special dessert happen. I would have to quickly explain . . .

* * *

12

(The Journey to My Recipe)

Moms loved reminding me, "your mind is cuckooier than an octopus juggling jars of jam while flying a rocket into the sun."

Yep, I had a dangerous imagination. This is why I hesitated to dig into my insane brain. Love makes you do dangerous things though. Within seconds of closing my eyes and exploring my mind for an epic dessert idea, I found myself hunting in a cookie cave.

Abruptly there appeared several beanie-wearing zombie geckos.

They chased me into a chocolate waterfall were I almost died a chocolate death. Thinking I escaped safely, my imagination ambushed me with a swarm of koalas dressed as creepy clowns. They tried drowning me in a raspberry lagoon. Maybe they wanted me to join them.

Now that I had the idea to make a chocolate raspberry pie, I raced to my moms' dessert shop — Loco For Choco.

The wackiest of my main bro-manos, Twitch, joined me to find Mrs. Yuki, aka the recipe master. We walked through a dark and dusty tunnel full of torches. When we finally found Mrs. Yuki, we interrupted her mid-killing a cockroach with a fly swatter. The bug turned out to be a ball of her back hair — I almost vomited.

She told us a long story about recipe masters guarding the secret ingredient from greedy ninjas for hundreds of years.

"So, what about the secret ingredient?" I said.

Mrs. Yuki faced me. "It's love."

"I knew that already."

"Hey, I don't get that many guests."

Twitch suddenly flicked a paper ninja star. "I am a *ninja*."

He whipped four more across the room — a real attention-getter.

Mrs. Yuki then sent us to see Günter Poffenbarger, the recipe librarian. When we arrived at his office, the sound of non-stop toilet flushing echoed through the hallway. Günter finally popped out of the bathroom and brought with him air pollution that peeled the wallpaper. Twitch and I snapped clothespins on our noses.

"Günter," I said, "can I please have the chocolate raspberry pie recipe?"

"How funnyz, I vuz just readingz it."

Günter dug the recipe from his back pocket and handed it to me.

OMG, had he been reading it while wrestling a turd python?

Luis Rodriguez

Günter opened a desk drawer, pulled out a hatchet, and lunged toward the bathroom. "For zee lovez of zee Deutchlandz, you vill not vin today!"

(Back to Now)

After that whole ordeal, my plan to impress the girl of my dreams arrived at a — *CRASH*. Everything went black. A vile voice woke me, phlegmy like a clogged drain.

"Hur hur hur hur. Did you guys see that epic fail? What a lame-o."

I opened my eyes and had to squint from a shimmering light.

"Lunelio, are you okay?"

Long hair and beautiful soft eyes loomed over me. "Are you an angel? Wait…am I dead?"

"No, silly — you're not dead." Viorica's blurred image came into focus.

"Not yet," said Bola.

"Ignore him, he's acting like a jerk."

Stars sparkled around my head. "Do I owe you my life?"

Viorica blushed. "Silly boy, how hard did you hit your gourd?"

Her angel-silk hands caressed my scalp.

"Hur hur hur," shouted the giant sewer gremlin. "Uh-oh Viorica, looks like he is dumber than before. Next time you get in my way lame-elio, you and your gross white hair are going to wake up in a coffin or somethin."

Luis Rodriguez

I opened my mouth to respond and instead watched Viorica's head snap *Exorcist*-style toward Bola.

"That is enough out of you."

She glared at the failed-steroid-experiment — machetes zipping from her eyes. Bola staggered back.

Like a magician, Math appeared out of nowhere. "Bola, you have made your message clear. Lunar is ready to get outta here."

A crowd had formed and some of the spectators spoke up.

"I don't know what crawled up Bola's butt and died, but he is always harassing people."

"Yeah, what a *jerk*, he knocked over Lunelio for no reason."

As quick as a chainsaw cuts, Bola turned and faced the crowd. "Who said that?"

Only the sound of crickets holding their breath could be heard.

"That's what I thought."

Again Math stepped in. "Hey Bola, take a chill-pill. Everything is all right, no need to start a fight —"

"Hey, loser friend of lame-elio, don't tell me what to do."

Nostrils flared, Bola paced up to Math, psychotic blood-thirsty bull's face skewed in Math's dark reflective shades. That horrible, greasy stomach bumped my friend — who flew backward into the gawkers, walking stick clattering to the floor. His clothes shone with rancid grease.

"*Hold up,*" Math cried. "That is *enough*. You're acting like a violent punk. Do you really wanna earn you the reputation of a greasy skunk?"

Bola's menacing shadow towered over Math. "Maybe I do, blind boy."

I struggled to my feet, ignored the screaming bruise on my butt-cheek. I needed to get my bromigo's back. Arms crossed, Math kept his stance.

"You need to *back off!*" Viorica roared.

Bola turned — anxiety surged into my gut.

"Or what? You gonna rescue blind-boy and the white-haired freak from mean old Bola or somethin?"

Those demonic eyes speared us with evil. Terrifying silence deafened me. A standoff, just like in the Wild West movies! Tumbleweeds of lunch debris rolled by. Bola's knuckles suddenly cracked, and goosebumps dotted my arms. I'm pretty sure even my bone marrow quivered. Viorica maintained her death-stare — raised a furious finger at the bully. "*No one* is fighting today."

Bola smirked. My stomach churned with gut bubbles.

"Hur hur hur. Lame-elio and his blind loser friend gonna let a girl fight their fights? You better change their diapers first or somethin."

"Thank you for sharing," Viorica snapped back. "Are you done being a jerk?"

Bola's leering expression of triumph beamed as if he'd just won first-prize for Ugliest Kid in the Hood. This had gone waaay too far. My mind and heart raced as I trotted clumsily toward Bola. "Your bullying is uncool and unwanted. Now, go make diarrhea out of someone else's day and leave us *alone*."

Spectators cheered me on. "*Tell* Bola what's what. Yeah!"

Bola's teeth clenched, nose scrunched, and fists raised. "*HAAARRRRREEEERR.*" His rabid-animal growl ripped the air in a wave of rotten butt-breath.

"You mess with a shark prepare to get eaten or somethin."

"Bola," I said, "was that supposed to be your 'shark snarl'? That all you got? Dummy, sharks don't snarl—Google it."

The crowd—led by Math—rewarded my snark with an "*Oooooouuuuuu.*"

Viorica shook her head. I shrugged. Whose side was she on anyway?

Bola erupted with the murderous tone of a thousand imploding bullies. "I'm. . . *not* a dummy. . . *you* are."

"Wow, nice comeback. Take a break so your brain doesn't go into a coma," I said.

Before I could chuckle at my joke, a behemoth hand gripped my rib cage like a fleshy vise. My lungs locked up.

"You're dead, lame-elio."

I could hear my bones crackling for mercy.

"*Stop,*" cried Viorica, "you're *hurting* him!"

She yanked his oily ear. My senses blurred, lungs oxygen-starved. Words seemed to float from her mouth to his ear. I couldn't hear anything, and silver specks glittered in my vision. Speaking of eyes, Viorica's glowed. I swear it!

Bola released me. Disgustingly, he massaged his head and staggered as if dizzy. Man, I hoped so!

Math lunged — whipped his cane karate-style at Bola.

"Keep this up," Math warned, powerful voice demanding attention, "you drunken buffoon, and you'll be seen as nothing but a dangerous *goon*. Instead, use honor as your fuel. . ."

The cafeteria dropped into dead silence.

"Face-off in a break dance duel," Math finished.

Shocked, the crowd shuddered. Wait, had my bro-slice just given me a death sentence? Didn't duels always end with someone, like, *dead*? What was Math thinking? Split-second bloodsucking thoughts buzzed in my mind. I hoped Math had a plan. "Time — three pee-em *sharp*," he went on. "Place — behind El Desmadre Taqueria."

Confused, Bola peered at me. "Breakdance duel?"

The crowd came back to life. "*You* heard *him, breakdance challenge. Yeaaah!*"

It felt killer to breathe again. I joined in. "*Yeah,* Bola, what's wrong? Too *pollo frito* for the challenge?"

At this, Viorica shook her head. Oh bleepin'
bleep, I must have looked *so* immature. Note to self:
learn when to shut my trap.

Bola nonchalantly (so he thought) puffed out
his chest, cracked his neck side-to-side. "Whatever,
white-haired freak and blind boy. I'll be there.
Viorica, bring a coffin for your girl-friends or
somethin. Ha!"

Viorica defiantly sneered at him, eyes fixing
fearfully on mine. They confirmed that Math had
ordered my death with extra sauce and I had gone
along with it.

The cafeteria floor abruptly shook.

Bola stomped away like a T.rex one week into a
vegetarian diet.

* * *

A Short Selfie-Biography, Just in Case I'm Murdered

I walked to study hall, and a thought wedged into my brain. As of today, death could be waiting around the corner and behind my favorite Mexican restaurant

My imagination bled raw fear. Anguished thoughts; despair. Would Bola not abide by the rules of the dance-off, instead rip me to shreds? That morbid bleep prompted me to write a selfie-final-goodbye-ography, dedicated to my family and crew.

Dear Familia and Bro-manos,

I once believed life to be a guaranteed box of crispy homemade tacos. Then a demon nearly ate me, my abuelita died, and my pops vanished. After today, if all goes wrong, I will be joining them both. I missed them…

I definitely won't miss people feeling sorry for me. Neighbors and random people would see a kid with a marshmallow white mop on his head and then talk to me like a helpless puppy. At first, I enjoyed it. I would get a hand-full of lollipops at every grocery store, cut the line at amusement parks, and teachers let me hand in homework late. I thought I had a pretty sweet deal. Then I got older and the cuteness of it all expired. People would cross the street when they'd see me, families would whisper behind my back, and kids would laugh me. It sucked being the

Luis Rodriguez

weirdo on the block. I sometimes felt a like a zombie or a Frankenstein. My gravestone should read, **Looked like a freakish old man, but had a dab-tastic heart.**

Maybe that's why I got into horror movies. I missed the Friday terror flick nights. My pops and I would turn off all the living room lights, jump on the couch, and flip through Netflix. We would scan through the horror section to find the most donkey dumb movies. Our top favorites were movies about bloodthirsty snowmen, sinister leprechauns, a homicidal Pinocchio, killer clowns from space, and a psychotic turkey looking for vengeance on Thanksgiving Day. The scariest parts of our movie nights were my dad's oily popcorn farts. If my pops could fart colors it would have looked like 4th of July. Huge PFFFTS filled up the room. I would yell at him.

"Pops, you gotta stop popping that butt corn. You're killing me old man."

He would laugh and rush to the bathroom. "If you hear me screaming it is because I'm being attacked by the – KILLER TOILET. Coming soon to a theater near you."

I then would grab my moms' Bible and respond. "Take this with you or else your next flush might be your last."

We would explode into crunchy balls of laughter even though we'd rehearsed this a thousand times. These were the moments feeling like a freak melted away.

It had been 9 months since my dad had disappeared on one of his newspaper assignments. He worked for the most famous news company, ABC World News Tonight.

I got used to him leaving for weeks and even months at a time. I didn't like it, but I felt proud of my pops. He would always bring back gifts: teddy bear voodoo dolls, troll teeth, blessed wooden stakes that were used to kill zombies, pirate ship coins, and medallions embedded with ancient lettering I couldn't understand. He once had brought me a shrunken head. It was damn cool but gave me the creeps. I kept it in our attic. I remember his famous peanut butter double chocolate pancakes. They were pretty much breakfast soaked in diabetes.

My pops took pictures for each story he worked on. He showed me pictures of cities destroyed by corrupt leaders, forgotten islands, ancient ruins, tribes that still lived in rainforests, science labs, up-coming inventions (such as a toilet that would rub your butt clean, a teleporting device that could send you across the world in seconds, and a breath mint that could make your farts smell like peppermint). My pops' had an epic job. He went on real adventures. "A hero always battles for the truth." he always said. My pops held the title of the most popular journalist in his office and we would often see him on tv. Now, I would sit down at night, watch re-runs of him, and cry.

The authorities gave up looking for my pops and the news company declared him dead. They found no clues, no blood, and no body. A sea of people filled the funeral home. I listened to a non-stop broken record of "sorry for your loss," "your papá is in a better place," "how sad for the poor kid," and I even remembered someone saying, "how tragic, does his kid have cancer?" The swarm of people made my stomach turn. I thought I might vomit. My little

Luis Rodriguez

sister slept on my tia's lap. My bro-migos were snagging some snacks in the dining area. Then my moms fell to her knees for the hundredth time and sobbed furiously. I started to suffocate. My eyes were red and raw from days of rubbing away tears. I thought I would dehydrate from all the crying. I looked over at my dad's coffin. It made me furious. The stupid wooden box laid empty. What was the damn point? How could my dad leave us like this? What a bleeping jerk. My thoughts were becoming a merry-go-round from hell. I wanted to run away. My eyeballs hungrily rummaged through the crowd for a door. Eureka. I had found a perfect escape. My knees bent and my legs were ready to sprint. Then a hand grabbed onto mine. The gently warm touch turned my legs to instant jelly. I looked behind me — Viorica. I looked at her beautiful dark-purple hair and exotic eyes. She opened her mouth to speak but no words came out. Viorica squeezed my hand.

"I don't know what to say Lunelio...I'm so sorry."

Next thing I knew, her arms were wrapped around me. Silently we stood. Me in her arms and tears cascading onto her shoulder. The pain from the hole in my soul, for the first time in months, had started to shrink. Later that night, I decided I felt love for the first time.

Now, I would probably never have the chance to tell her how I felt. In a couple of hours, Bola fists would crush me into a flesh-and-bones guacamole. Abruptly, the image of my moms at my pops funeral flashed back into my mind.
. .

Brrrring!

The school bell rang and I dropped my pencil. So many memories I left out; my fearless abuelita teaching me true magic, the day my moms scared off bullies with a chancla, and my annoying little sister. Who was I kidding? Why the bleep would anyone want to read this letter anyway? I quickly wiped away fresh tears.

I held the letter in my fingertips, balled it up, and trashed it.

* * *

An Annoying Weasel

On the way to science class, death and love spun circles in my brain. I felt like a science experiment. In one moment I floated on a chariot of sunshine, and the next I could hear an undertaker shoveling moist dirt onto my coffin.

"Yo, Lunar-eclipse." Math prodded my gut with his walking stick.

"Math, what's up?" He examined my face, probed its bone structure. My mug, distorted, and mirrored in his shades screamed drama.

"Lunar, you look like you're stuck in a paradoxical bubble with two forces pulling your mind in polar-opposite directions."

"Really, Math?"

The only person who could ever understand his nerd-talk was my nerd-cousin Chuy. "Translation please."

He smiled, showing off sparkly white teeth; licorice-colored hair bounced curlily.

"You have a lot on your mind; a combo of love and war."

"Actually, bro-slice, it's a combo of love and *death*."

"Yeah, man, today has been a bit heavy. Your moment with Viorica turned into a date with destiny.

But don't worry, the crew and I have your back. You ready to continue our experiment?"

Our experiment, *duh*. The perfect distraction to keep my mind off "things."

Math grabbed our tray of plants. I could see some already sprouting tall and others still hiding in dirt. Math's geek-inspired idea borrowed from a Japanese scientist named Dr. Masaru Emoto — the scientist dude put rice and water into three jars. For a month straight, he said "thank you" to one, gave the other the stink-eye while calling it an idiot, and the third he totally ignored. What happened at the end of the month was nuttier than a hairless crossed-eyed mole rat. The first jar of rice got bubbly and burped up a sweet aroma; pretty much a rice soda. The second turned rat-turd black, and the third vomit-green. The results made my brain want to retire. How was that possible? Luckily, I had my bro-mano to explain it.

"Lunar, the intention behind our words carries powerful energy. You focus on the good and it grows. You focus on the bad and—"

"*Heheheehdidydeeheee.*"

An annoying high-pitched giggle ambushed my flashback.

"Wow, I just got an inside look into the life of lame losers. Your lives would make the lamest reality show that no one would watch. *Hehehdiheedyheedeeheee.*"

Wilfredo, aka Weasel, surprise-attacked us with insult grenades!

Weasel was one of Bola's goons.

Whenever his frightful mug popped up like a pimple, that meant he had a message from Bola. We called him Weasel because his personality matched the name. I also imagined his parents deserted him in a forest at birth. Abandoned in the dark for days, until a clan of foul weasels found him. Deciding (accurately) the child was too ugly to eat, instead they raised him.

Weasel's ginger-red hair puffed up in curls like a disheveled clown and he laughed louder than a hyena. A gaping smile stretched his mouth like cookie dough — pictured in the dictionary under "creepy." Worse, Weasel had a wicked lazy eye which pondered the outside world like a drunk gnat in a fish bowl. Too, he loved his tummy hole, and infamously picked at it no matter who might be around to witness. It could easily cradle two medium-sized meatballs. How did I know? Weasel's gut reliably peeked from under his too-small shirt, and I'm sure he used that belly hole to store leftover food. His yellowed fingernail scooped out a treat, then plugged into his nose allowing Weasel to savor the aroma. For the grand finale, he nibbled delicately at the *food* as if dining at an expensive restaurant. Thinking about that, I almost barfed! "Math, is he talking to you?" I said. "I can't tell, one eye is pointed at me and the other is bouncing around like a bedbug on caffeine."

"Lunar, I really don't know. I find his lazy eye distracts even my blindness." Weasel favored us with that sinister grin, and held out a note. "Yeah, uh, whatever you lame bleep-heads—you guys are too lame even to take seriously. I'm here to deliver a message to the soon-to-be-deceased. *Heedeehedeehedee.*"

I hesitated to grab it, and took a soft hit in the ribs courtesy of Math's ninja-like reflexes.

I snatched the note. "Thanks, Weasel. We just ran out of toilet paper and this will come in handy."

Weasel held his twisted smile. "I'll make sure to deliver that message to my compadre."

"We have received the message, now be gone pestering errand boy. The consequences, I promise, you will not enjoy." Like a samurai, Math whipped his walking stick in defense stance. When Math began to rhyme that meant *back off or else.*

Weasel retreated several steps. "Whatever—blind boy...like *you* could even hit me."

Smack. Math's walking stick struck Weasel's shin.

"*Ouch,* you jerk."

Math stepped closer. "I will not say it again. Be *gone* minion. If this warning you fail to comprehend, a more painful one I will send."

Confused, Weasel cringed with fear. "Huh? Did you just speak—English, Spanish...or *loser*? Anyway,

I can't leave until I see the white-haired dead boy read the message. Bola's orders."

Weasel crossed his arms and retreated farther.

"It's ok, Math, I'll read the note."

Swallowing my fear, I sensed sticky sweat-beads under my pits and unfolded the note. Involuntarily, as I read, Bola's gruesome voice boomed in my head.

WIT HARED FREEK, DIS IS UH FRENLY RAMINDR OF UR FUNRAL TUDAY. BEE REDDY FOR DA DANS DULL. AFTR I BEET U...I WILL BEET YOU! HOOP U TULD UR PARINTS U LUV EM TUDAY."

Poorly drawn on the note, an etched tombstone read: *LOSR*. A blob-shaped figure peed on what I guessed must be Yours Truly's grave.

My insides frosted, as if icicles clutched the fragile organs. Glancing up in horror, I got treated to the sight of Weasel's long pinky fingernail extracting from his belly button some crusty brown substance, and spooning it into his mouth. I fought the urge to vomit. Weasel's beady gaze met mine.

"Look at the bright side, at least you won't be a loser anymore. Dead men can't be losers — they're *dead. Heedeehedeehedeehehe."*

An ancient inferno of anger surged from my soul, melted fear. "You tell that Bola de grasa that after I'm done kicking his butt, I'm gonna teach him how to read and write. Then his messages won't look like they're written by a drunk baby." Smoke blasted

Theory of Relativity

"You've got to ask yourself one question. Do you feel lucky? Do ya, punk?"

The words jarred me—my weighty history book fell and pancaked my toes like a cartoon character's. That's how it felt!

Behind me chuckled none other than Hollywood, the final piece of the Picasso that was our crew of compadres, master of random movie and tv-inspired quotes.

"Dude," I said, "where the bleep have you been hiding?"

Hollywood grinned, trendy red-framed glasses glinting, and plucked a comb from his back pocket to sharpen his slick do. *"You talkin to me?"*

"Um, *duh*, who else am I—"

"Hey, you talkin to me?" He peered blankly as if he hadn't heard.

"Hollywood, snap out of your movie moment—you're stuck on replay." I snapped my fingers before his face.

Winking, he handed me a note: *Bro-mano, I hear we have to plan out your funeral today. I need you to put in your will that I get to keep your dead body. My plan is to have you stuffed. Next, I will put a motor in you that would make your dead arms move so we can still dab together.*

Glaring, I shook my head. He spilled cackles over the twisted message.

"Hollywood, good to know you have my back."

My bro-ski popped back into character-mode as the Terminator.

"Do not worry. If you want to live, come with me. I'll *crush* Bola with my bare fists, while juggling porcupines on fire, and standing on a bleeping Viking's sword! *Arrrruugghhhlll!*"

I couldn't hold back laughter. "Just help me keep it a dance-duel." I broke into moonwalk-mode, sliding robotically across the floor.vThe principal's sudden voice exploded through the hallway. "Bola, how *dare* you act as if you are innocent! Have the decency to admit to your crime after getting caught red-handed!"

A gruesome voice protested. "It wasn't me. I'm innocent. I didn't do *nuthin.*"

Mr. Neville's face flushed chilli pepper red — he looked ready to explode. "*Poppycock.* You are suspended. You...spineless...deviant — *thief!*"

Bola's massive head emerged, and I could see he struggled against crying. "Well I . . . I . . . Don't care, you cara de nalga!"

Shocked, my bro-mano and I gaped at each other. Man — only Bola would have the pecans to call the principal butt face. *Oooo's* and *oooh's* cut the air. In the crowd someone yelled, "Daaaamn. Principal Neville just got *roasted.*" A tidal wave of laughter flooded the hallways. Teachers moved like referees to break up the mob of kids.

"Get your bleepin hands off me, losers. I di-di-didn't do *nuthin*!"

Goosebumps shivered on my forearms.

Myself, Hollywood, and countless witnesses watched all the security guards and staff tackle—and tie up—Bola as if a deranged ape. Dragged across the floor, he left a juicy grease stain all the way to the front doors. Like an Olympic curler, the school engineer followed, mopping Bola's rancid body gravy. Mr. Neville stood, fists to his waist Superman-style. Sunlight illuminated the tie's lime polka dots and bird-nest toupee. The principal looked almost tough. In Terminator-mode, Hollywood declared, "*Has-ta la vis-ta, Bo-la.*"

My heart exhaled with relief. "The forces of destiny must have taken pity on me, Hollywood. I get to live to see another day."

Hollywood nodded. "Mama always said life was like a box of chocolates. You never know which one will be your last."

He smiled, as if that anecdote were reassuring. I grinned at the thought of getting a break from the sewer-beast's harassment.

Time froze. Fingertips, soft and furtive, teased my back with subtle electricity. An aroma sweeter than fairy burps tickled my nose—Viorica appeared out of nowhere. My insides foamed into a milkshake.

"Lunelio, are you okay? I was worried. Thought you two had gotten into a fight."

Our gazes met. Lost in those eyes, I held my breath.

"Lunelio?" Viorica shook me by the shoulders.

". . . Hey . . ."

"Are you ok?" "Yeah…think so? Unless I'm dreaming. If so, please don't wake me."

"Do you plan on making some quesadillas with that cheese?"

I shrugged; gave a goofy grin.

She narrowed those magic eyes. "Tomorrow you're sitting with me during lunch."

"I am?"

"Do you have a problem with that?"

My chest thumped — was I going to have a heart attack?

Scrrreeeccchhh.

Viorica jumped in front of me as Twitch zoomed toward us — halted at the last second barely an inch away.

"Sorry guys, didn't mean to scare you. I gotta get some new tires on this turbo-mobile."

I shot a look his way that said, *did-you-really-almost-flatten-the-girl-of my-dreams?* He shrugged apologetically. I faced Viorica. "Are you ok?"

She winked. "This is not my first near-death experience."

"This is Twitch," I said, "the craziest wheelchair driver ever."

Stupidly smiling, he offered a hand.

Viorica clasped it and they shook. "Thanks for not running us over."

Hollywood prodded my side with a bony elbow.

"Oh, sorry. I was *bout* to introduce my calm bro-mano before this lump-head almost killed us. This is Hollywood, the whiz of reinventing movie quotes."

"Nice to meet you, Hollywood. Do all of you have nicknames?"

Before Hollywood could reply Twitch interrupted, babbling a mile a second. "Yeah, I had to rush over here to make sure Lunar-eclipse still lived. Dude, I almost lost my marbles with worry."

Viorica chuckled. "I was worried about **Lun-ar-eclipse** too." Again she laughed, and my face flushed.

Twitch rambled. "Man, that Bola sure has some *bolas*. I heard they found him in a room with the walls full of blood. I heard he tried to eat Principal Neville, ugly wig and all. I heard it took 20 guards to take him down."

Hollywood and I shook our heads. The gossip bug had spread fast. "Bro-mano, all that gossip is a bunch of bull-plop, me and Hollywood saw the whole thing."

Twitch's eyelids popped up like window curtains. "No *way*. What the heck balls happened? Spill the beans already."

Hollywood huffed. "Patience, grasshopper."

"Okay Twitch," I said, "before you have an aneurysm, we saw Principal Neville savagely yell at Bola for stealing something, I think. Then had the orangutan dragged out of the school like a greasy rag."

"I wonder what Bola got caught stealing?" said Viorica.

"Who knows, probably—"

Twitch sliced through my sentence. "I know, I know. I heard they found him in the library trying to open a book. He got frustrated, started to eat the people around him, and spattered the walls with blood. He took his victims' eyeballs to make a necklace—a souvenir. Bola likes the way eyeballs shine. Anyway, stealing people's eyes is illegal."

My ears wanted to leap from my head and slap Twitch's face.

"C'mon Twitch, so is *killing* people. We would have seen Bola covered in blood and carrying eyeballs."

A skinny kid with owl eyes and gapped teeth barged into our conversation, barfed out more stupid gossip.

"I heard Bola became bored while trapped in the library because he forgot how to open a door. So, he grabbed random victims and started tearing out their limbs and snapping the arm bones into the leg holes and the leg bones into the arm holes like human Legos—"

Immediately another kid ambushed the discussion. "Yeah? I heard Bola decided the only way he could pass this year was by eating a nerd's brain. So, he went to the library where he knew he would find a lot of them. The library is like their church. Bola next burst through the doors and twisted off some nerds' heads, dug through their nerdy necks, and devoured each brain like creamy custard."

A herd of other students gathered, trapped us in an avalanche of gossip. Twitch switched his wheelchair into turbo-mode; Hollywood jumped into its basket and they reversed out of the madness. I grabbed Viorica and we escaped by army-crawling under the crowd.

"You guys made it," squealed Twitch. "That crowd totally lost its marbles."

"I agree," said Viorica, "this is getting ridiculous."

Hollywood blew out a huge sigh. "I feel like I'm taking crazy pills."

Again that weird electricity jolted me, and I saw Viorica's hand clasping mine—so did my bro-manos. Hollywood whistled and awkwardly shifted his head. Twitch, for some reason, sang. "Lunar and Viorica sitting in a tree, k-i-s-s-i-n-g. First comes loves, then comes marriage, then—"

"*Twitch,*" I snapped.

"When you guys get married," he went on, "I'd better be your best man."

Hollywood shrugged, legs dangling in the wheelchair's basket. Then they both zipped away Nascar-style.

Softly Viorica squeezed my hand, and our fingers meshed. I pictured one of Chuy's posters titled *Einstein's Theory of Relativity*. When I asked Viorica what that meant, she said *some moments (like waiting in line for a roller coaster) feel as if they last forever, and others (like riding your favorite roller coaster) feel like shards of a second.* Turning, I floated into her almond eyes . . . so caught up in her magic that if she told me to break into an orphanage and slap a nun, I probably would have.

Viorica waved her hands before my face. "Earth to Lunelio. Are you in the middle of a Lunar-eclipse right now?"

Love-trance popped, I tried to play it off. "Welcome to Lunar Burgers, may I take your order?"

"Very funny, mister fast-food. Tomorrow, lunch?"

"Yes, yes, and yes." Oh bleep, that sounded lame.

Viorica smiled and nearly gave my eyeballs diabetes.

"Good. In the meantime, stay away from Bola's goons." Again she squeezed my hand—more electricity. Her pupils dilated as she peered at me. Were her eyes glowing, hiding some secret behind them?

I blinked and she was gone.

It Came Back

Only a few days of school remained, and we were anxious to be done. We roasted under an arm-pit-sauna hot temp. Bird poop on car windows sizzled like eggs frying. I decided to stop at my cousin Chuy's house; their air-conditioner blasted arctic air.

I found her typing away, near the end of her senior year research paper. A physics genius (aka a NERD), she and Math could blab for hours. Truth was, I loved my cousin, and her nerdiness sometimes made me jealous. Scattered all over her desk were notebooks with titles like *Einstein's theories*, *The 4th Dimension*, *Atoms*, *Quantum Equations*, and a whole mess more nerd books with names I couldn't pronounce. As Chuy splashed a geek tsunami of ideas all over her paper, I practiced for the dance duel.

My feet memorized and I rehearsed last summer's final dance routine. The mastermind was my crazy Scottish break-dance coach. At any moment Math would call me with the info on Bola's suspension. Maybe they would exile him for life. Nah—I wasn't born pooping leprechauns. With all this on my brain, I still couldn't stop thinking about Viorica. Why had she asked me to lunch? Did she know I had feelings for her? Maybe this was a trick? It wouldn't be the first time a girl pretended to like

Luis Rodriguez

me, as a prank. In third grade at my old school, this mean girl named Bonnie set me up. She wrote me a note saying I should ask her to be my girlfriend. I thought, why not? I did, she turned me down, spilled chocolate milk on my head and loudly exclaimed, "Now your gross white hair has some *color*."

The whole cafeteria had laughed. I just couldn't imagine Viorica being that heartless. Maybe she felt sorry for me. Maybe she just saw me as a pathetic kid with white hair, no dad, and — A knock sounded on the door.

I followed Chuy downstairs; checked the peep-hole and could see a hooked witch-nose — scary.

"*Dude*," I warned, "don't open that door."

Chuy ignored me and opened it. Her neighbor Nachismo Frutos stood there. I called him the Nacho Man because he smelled of old cheese (this annoyed Chuy).

"Good day Armanda," — he motor-mouthed a hundred miles per hour — "how are you — that's great — you're getting so big — almost done with school — bet you will be a scientist one day — I need a *big* favor."

"Sure, Mr. Frutos. Is everything okay?"

Suspiciously he peered from side to side. "Yes . . . No . . . I must leave right away."

Chuy's eyebrows arched. "Oh, okay. Going on vacation?"

Mr. Frutos rebounded. "I can't tell you that. No. It might . . . not be safe — it is better you don't know."

My creepy-o-meter clanged. Danger! The Nacho Man's odd behavior and dangling nose hairs gave me the blazing heebie-jeebies — tempted me to slam the door in his face. There followed an awkward pause.

Chuy pushed for forward. "The favor?"

"Yes of course how silly of me — I need you to take care of my precious Pebbles."

Chuy raised a hand and gnawed a thumbnail. Her spidey-senses must've gone off! Underneath the Nacho Man's sour cheese odor lurked a darker taint of trouble.

"I don't know, Mr. Frutos. Pebbles is a Great Dane; pretty much the biggest dog I've ever seen. She's also really old."

He nodded. "Yes, eleven years *is* quite ancient for a dog."

"Well, I'm drafting my final paper on quantum theory, and right now that's enough responsibility for me."

"Quantum que? Of course, I will pay. I have here a travel voucher to fly first class anywhere in the world. Take it, it's yours."

The Nacho Man stuffed an envelope into Chuy's hand. She opened it, scanned the paper closely until a smile dawned.

The Nacho Man gave Chuy six months of dog food, supplies, and pet insurance in case Pebbles got sick. Sniffling and teary-eyed, the panicky old man hugged Pebbles and stormed off. To where? Chuy and I had no idea. The Nacho Man, though, had vowed to return in three months.

Chuy shrugged. "Looks like it's just the three of us, old girl."

Pebbles blankly regarded us, and like some weathered grandma shuffled toward the living room carpet, plopped down, farted, and closed her eyes.

* * *

Later that week my family and I dropped by for a visit.

I barged into Chuy's bedroom. "What's up, cuuuuuz."

"*Aaaaah,*" Chuy screamed. A Stephen Hawking book flew toward me—smacked into my head. Unbalanced, I bounced off the wall and landed on my stomach. "Ouch!"

"*OMG*—Lunelio, are you okay?"

Chuy ran over and cradled me like a child.

Stunned, I beheld her as if about to take my last breath. "*Avenge me . . .*"
She rubbed my head. "Get up and let me examine you for bruises."

After she apologized a jillion times, and gave me several big hugs, we ended up in the kitchen where Chuy cooked me up some homemade hot chocolate and we opened some real talk.

"Lunelio, I need you to keep a secret."

My insides gurgled with excitement. Chuy was about to tell me something *serious*. "It's me you're talking to, Chuy. I'm like a safe inside a sunken pirate ship."

So, I listened to my cuz as she nervously spilled all the creepy beans. This story made my hands rattle like loose teeth inside a dirty tin can. The hot chocolate I tried sipping spattered over my feet. Chuy, being a complete mess, made it worse. Her pale face worried me, as if she might faint.

"Breathe, Chuy, *breathe*." I rested a gentle hand on her shoulder.

* * *

Chuy's Story

After a week of dog-sitting, bizarre things began to happen, starting with random cellphone calls. I would answer with a *"Hello?"*

Nothing on the other end but what sounded like someone breathing. On Friday night, my *Star Wars* ring-tone woke me. Drool had spotted my quantum mechanics textbook.

"Gross . . ."

"Lunelio, don't interrupt."

"Sorry."

The cellphone rang again and I answered. *"Hello?"*

No answer. "Hellooo?"

On the other end, I could hear the disturbing sound of what sounded like someone chewing meat—wet and nasty. *"I want the dooooog."*

Whoever it might be was playing gruff, words choked out as if through the ancient rot of a mummy . . . or something far from human.

I nearly peed my paints, dropped the phone, and ran to my parents' room. They were convinced it must be a friend pulling a prank.

But after a week of more haunting and mysterious creeper calls, I had my number changed. A few weeks went by and the creepster-calls stopped.

I finally got back into my paper-writing groove: studying, watching documentaries, and taking care of the old girl. This is when Pebbles really started to worry me. She did nothing but sleep all day. The old girl's eyes rarely opened. When they did, they seemed to sag with sorrow. I thought she might get sick without a bit of exercise. So, I tried playing fetch, Frisbee, tug of war, and chase the neighbor's cat. I went so far as purposely leaving trails of food to get the elderly canine moving. Nothing worked. Pebbles' daily routine included napping, peeing, eating very little, barely pooping, and napping again. Even falling asleep mid-poop.

"Chuy, you could have left that detail out."

Anyway, I read an article about astronauts landing a space probe on an asteroid, when my computer notification beeped. A Facebook message popped up.

"Hello Armanda."

While laser-focused on the article, I absentmindedly clicked. "Hello right back at ya." I usually always block rando messages.

It beeped again.

"I'm hungry Armanda..."

Again, I wasn't paying attention and replied, "Go make yourself a snack."

Another beep.

"Ooohhhh, I like snacks hee hee hee..."
I finally realized I had been messaging with a rando. I moved the mouse to click block user when several more beeps spat from the computer.

"HOW ABOUT I SNACK ON YOUR FLESH? I CAN ALREADY HEAR YOUR LIMBS BURST AT THE THOUGHT OF ME TEARING THEM FROM THEIR SOCKETS. WHAT A TASTY SOUND THAT WOULD MAKE, DON'T YOU THINK?"

I fell off my chair and began to dry heave.

More horrible beeps.

"I WANT THE BLEEPING DOG ARMANDA. I CAN SMELL YOUR FLESH FROM HERE ARMANDA. HEE HEE HEE. DO YOU WANT TO DIE ARMANDA?"

I powered off my computer and screamed all the way to my parents' room.

Several sleepless nights passed with me quivering under my blankets. I refused to touch that cursed computer. My parents decided to recycle it, and buy me a new laptop with an expensive firewall.

"Chuy, tell me the story is over."

"Lunelio, I *wish*."

The phone calls and Facebook messages were torture, but *yoga class* . . .

"Maybe I don't wanna hear this."

"Sorry Nelio, you have no choice."

After that day, nightmares of a strange tall man in a black coat chasing me had invaded my dreams. While awake, I constantly looked over my shoulders in class, in the library, on the bus, and — everywhere. Nothing seemed normal to me anymore and everyone looked suspicious. It felt trapped in a nightmare play where everyone schemed to scare me into an early grave. Mamá suggested I take some yoga classes to unwind and de-stress. Without a second thought, I dug into my closet, pulled out a mat, and drove to the neighborhood yoga studio. As soon as I stepped in, the comforting scent of sandalwood filled the warm air and calmed me.

"Time for some hot yoga folks," the yoga instructor declared, and upped the temperature.

My body became Silly Putty and I bent into the bridge, the cobra, the crane, the headstand, and the vicious pretzel.

"*Chuy* – you're making those poses up."

"*SSShusssh.* Stop interrupting."

Basically, I was kicking yoga butt. I noticed a man's reflection in the studio mirror. The very sight of him instantly paralyzed me. I wanted to simultaneously faint, scream, and pee myself. The man looked like a thing poorly disguised as a man. He…it – whatever, had bone-white skin, ashy stringy hair, and a grimy grey bread. Like a decaying Christmas tree, green chunks with maggots clung to the beard. It also wore sunglasses. Behind its black shades, I could see red glowing eyes. The man-thing smiled at me, exposing rows of long sharp teeth.

"Whoa – mega-grimy."

"Lunelio, it gets worse."

It wasn't even his soul-thirsty grin that scared me the most. I glanced back at the mirror; man-thing's stomach twitched and squirmed under his shirt – like small creatures were fighting to escape.

I grabbed my stuff and ran out the door.

Driving off, I peered into my rearview mirror. There he stood, outside the yoga studio. With a vile smirk gashing his face, he held up several bloody cats' tails.

"*No way!*" Hot chocolate spurted from my mouth.

"Lunelio, you're making a *mess*."

"Sorry Chu-ster, but this story leaped from rated-R to rated I-have-to-go-check-my-underwear."

Chuy visibly shook cleaning my mess.

"Ok, cuz, we need to come up with a plan."

* * *

We spent the entire day brainstorming how we might uncover the secret behind this super-scary stalker.

Chuy continued acting nuttier than a pack of peanuts on four shots of espresso.

She crazily wrote out math formulas on a dry-erase board. Watching her made my brain want to jump off a cliff.

I walked into the kitchen, poured some fresh watermelon juice, and glanced down Pebbles. Her ancient eyes blinked back at me. Into my mind popped a vision — her doggy funeral! Gathered around her coffin were old German Shepherds, pit bulls, Schnauzers, Beagles, and wiener dogs all dressed in black suits and dresses. Behind black veils, the females whimpered while a Chihuahua priest gravely spoke. After the funeral, they would stuff Pebbles and honor her in a museum. Chuckling at my own brain-movie, I stooped and petted the old girl. From her collar dangled a silver heart, shimmery and pure. A tiny keyhole almost escaped my sight.

I found a safety pin and probed the hole.

Nothing. Shrugging, I stepped away to take a wizz. *Zap.* An abuelita memory channeled into my brain. It dated from during my true magic training. Her secret scrolls were locked in a safe and she couldn't find the key. So abuelita used a spell to open the safe.

"Mijito," she had said, "one day this spell will come in handy for you too."

I closed my eyes, and whispered, *"Llave Autem Dei, Aperta."Bink.*

The heart-lock popped open and out fell a small shimmering key. *"Chuy."*

Chuy and I stared at the key. Short, thick, and had a unique three-dimensional jigsaw shape. It felt to be beckoning us.

"OMG Lunelio, you're a genius. How did you find this?"

"What can I say?" I boasted. "White hair is not the only thing I have in common with Einstein — aaah. Pebbles, what are you doing to my leg?"

I jerked back attempting to shake the ancient animal from humping my leg and fell. Startled, Chuy dropped the key into Pebbles' bowl of food. My butt thumped the floor and I immediately grasped a bottle of house cleaner and sprayed my violated leg.

"*Bad* old lady dog," I scolded. "These are my fav jeans and now I might have to burn them."

"Lunelio, stop being a big baby and help me find the key."

"Excuse me, Miss Insensitive, for being a little traumatized. I'll probably need some counseling after this is all over."

"Well, get in line mister."

I got off my sore buns and grabbed a fork. Pebbles slyly dipped her snout in the bowl and took a large bite.

"Noooooooo," I yelled.

"What is it?"

I watched her, and had to bite my lip. "Chuster, we are gonna need a pooper-scooper and a pair of walking shoes."

* * *

The sun's scorching breath screamed down on us. Chuy, Pebbles, and I melted as we walked toward the veterinarian's office. we hoped to motivate Pebbles to poop before we reached our destination. If that failed, we would initiate plan B: Dr. Coelho. Chuy called him the Dr. Dolittle of India because he had a reputation for saving dying animals — and he was from India.

I felt relieved.

"If anyone can get Pebbles to poop out the key," said Chuy, "it's Doc C."

"So how far of a walk are we looking at?"

"At least thirty minutes."

"Thirty minutes? Will Pebbles make it?"

Chuy peered at me with heavy eyes. "I sure *hope* so."

I glanced up at the burning hot sun, and down at Pebbles' panting tongue. My heart kamikazed into my gut. "Let's make sure we give the old girl plenty of water breaks."

Chuy nodded. After several blocks, Pebbles' parchment-paper eyelids fought to stay open. Meanwhile her paws dragged.

"Chuy, Pebbles looks like the doggie Grim Reaper is ready to give her a six-foot-deep dirt nap."

"Oh gosh, I'm in such a rush I —" she quickly poured water into the dog's mouth.

Pebbles slurped up the fluid as if she had been abandoned in the Sahara Desert.

"Lunelio, any sign of doggie poop?"

"Really? Since when am *I* on great-granny-dog dookie detail?"

"Lunelio, pleeeassse. You're my knight — my soldier — my hero."

"Stop kissing butt. I'll see if I find any black gold."

I dreadfully walked over to Pebbles' ancient buns, searched for fudge nuggets with the hope that one might hold our silver clue. I took out my telescope. Like an astronomer examining a black hole for the first time, I carefully examined one of the grossest areas in the universe.

Chuy smiled broadly. "Well, Galileo, any turd-lings?"

"No sign of chocolate gremlins."

She sighed. "I hope Doc C. is able to help us." She looked down at Pebbles and pleaded. "C'mon girl, we have to keep going—you can do it."

Eyes blinking with new life, the dog fought to not go into the light. I shook my head in pity, pictured Pebble's funeral again. We continued walking until reaching a busy street with a red-light. It lasted for a brief eternity. "By the time we get the green," I said, "she'll be dead."

"Lunelio, think positive. This old girl could use a rest." Chuy paused and pet the dog's balding bristly head.

Pebbles turned to us and smiled. Next, the dog plopped her wrinkly old body on the ground. She lay there like a sack of meat and bones wrapped in a soggy gray towel.

"Good girl," Chuy purred, stroking Pebbles.

The light changed. "Walk signal."

Energetically, I marched several steps ahead. *Krkrkrkrkrr.* A blood-curdling dragging sound paused me.

"*Oh no,*" Chuy cried.

I turned to see Chuy on her knees checking Pebble's pulse. Immediately I raced to her side. "Let me try restarting her heart." I placed my hands where I thought her heart might be, and pressed in counts of three.

After a few moments, Pebbles' began to move. "It's a miracle," I shouted.

Pebbles farted, her eyes closed, face fell to the side, and tongue dangled lifelessly.

"Oh no, she's dead!" Chuy and I yelled.

There we were, stuck with a large dead dog, a mysterious key hiding in her poop tube, under the unforgiving sun, and clueless what to do.

So we panicked.

Frantically, we dragged Pebbles' body to an alley leaving behind a bread-crumb trail of fur patches.

I felt hopeless. "Chu-ster, what are we gonna do? Huh?"

Chuy looked down at me as if dazed, eyes like two dark marbles lost in the treacherous sea of what just happened. "I . . . dunno . . . Lunelio…"

"We have to figure *something* out, before…we get *arrested* for killing this poor dog."

Chuy stood frozen. "I . . . dunno . . . I . . . dunno . . . I . . . dunno . . . "

Smack. I slapped her face. "*Snap* out *of it.*"

My cuz came to, and the nerd-looking hamster in her head began running at light-speed. "I *got* it

Lunelio. We can call an Uber and stick with plan B and head for the vet. *He'll* know what to do."

"Chuy, do you have the Uber app?"

"Nope."

"So *now* what?"

"The bus. It's one block away."

"Sounds great. I'll just drape this thousand-pound dog over my shoulder."

"Oh gosh, Lunelio, I'm not thinking clearly. We need to hide Pebbles in something."

"Or we can look like psychos."

Chuy ignored my sarcasm and scanned our perimeter, quickly pointed to the end of the alley. "The Dumpster®."

* * *

I never thought this day would come.

Chuy insisted I would find something we could hide Pebbles in. So I rolled up my sleeves and took a Scrooge McDuck dive right into a lagoon of garbage.

"Find anything yet?"

"Of course I have. But it's so awesome drowning in garbage, I just wanna simmer in it a bit longer simply for the memories."

Fishing through the garbage, I realized gazing at Pebbles' butt hadn't been so bad. After all, there were many treasures: soiled diapers so heavily packed they could be used as a poop grenade, rotted food wiggling with happy maggots, a large white tooth (I kept it to make some Tooth-Fairy money), and some crusty yellowed toenail clippings the size of potato chips. I considered keeping them as clues to track down Bigfoot (*he's real I tells ya*). Otherwise, nothing large enough to hide Pebbles.

"*Eureka.*"

I heard Chuy as I burrowed out of trash-topia. She pulled on an old suitcase wedged behind the Dumpster. I immediately pushed the metal trash box with all my muscle juice. Chuy yanked free the moldy piece of luggage. The commotion woke a colony of rats. They scampered and squeaked wildly as if they had just drunk from a tub of my uncle's tequila. We screamed and ran in circles. Trust me, it only *sounds* funny.

After several minutes, the charcoal-colored rodents gathered in one corner of the alley and formed into a furry black ball. We gingerly stepped away, nervous they might call out to their hundreds of friends and eat us alive. They began a loud, repetitive hiss.

"Oh no, Chuy — they're sending an alert to have us ambushed. I think we're on the dinner menu."

"Sssh Lunelio, stay calm."

I scanned my whirling brain for one of my abuelita's spells, but couldn't focus. "Chuy, am I hallucinating?"

She didn't answer. Her mouth gaped wide enough to swallow a grapefruit.

The rats!

With their bodies — I kid you not — they were spelling out words. *D* . . . *A* . . .   *N* . . . Then *G* . . . *E* . . . *R* . . . The rats continued. *I* . . . *S* . . . *C* . . . *O* . . . Their hissing grew even louder. *M* . . . *I* . . . *N* . . . *G*.

My knees weakened into rubbery blobs, and I feared toppling into *them*.

Chuy noticed — grabbed my arm.

I dared a glance behind, saw we were only steps away from the alley entrance. I turned back, and the rats were gone! Just . . . gone.

"OMG Chuy, we're still alive." And my pants — miraculously — still were dry.

She hugged me. "Lunelio, did we just hallucinate that episode?"

"I *wish*, and nope!"

"There must be a logical explanation."

"Nope."

Chuy gnawed her lips. "Let's get us and Pebbles the h-word *out* of here."

Chuy sat atop the case and zipped it as I mushed Pebble's head and tail inside. Bones cracked — I accidentally yanked out fur clumps. The dog's body bulged from each side of the suitcase, and the entire deal dragged as we pushed. People gawked at our struggles, and Chuy smiled nervously.

"What in the blazes just happened Chu-ster?"

"Lunelio, I can't wrap my cerebellum around it . . . the rats were sending us a *message*."

"I know, 'danger is coming.' What the hell does *that* mean?" No need to swear."

"If ever there was a time —"

"Oh no, the zipper!" Its painfully clenched teeth, stressed beyond design limits by a dead dog, were about to pop like a can of biscuit dough. Pins and needles sharply fizzed in my chest, and I gripped the case using both hands, pointed it toward the sun, and whispered ancient true-magic words. "Cerradura Impervius."

Chuy's eyes favored me. "You just cast — one of abuelita's spells?"

"Yep, the spell of impenetrability. It just woke up inside of me." "Really, what does it do?"

"If it works, the suitcase will stay sealed until I uncast the spell."

Chuy's gaze dropped. "My parents never let abuelita teach me her magic. They called it witchery. I still remember abue's words. *True magic is your birthright mija, it is in your blood, no one could take that from you.*"

"*I* can teach you."

Chuy nodded. "Sure. But let's get out of here before something even stranger happens."

Finally, after swimming in sweat — a bus stop.

* * *

We did our best to look normal and blend in with the rest of the folks. A mother with curly big 80s hair holding a double baby carriage entertained her two infants. A high school kid wore giant headphones blasting music and quaking his whole body. This tall lanky man, bearded and wearing shades, black suit, white gloves, and a black brimmed hat, clutched a Bible in one hand and sported a clerical collar. A priest headed to a funeral? The poor guy must have been melting.

So many thoughts swirling in my mind . . . that bleeping key stuck inside Pebbles, those bleeping rats and their freaky message, and then my abuelita. I felt her voice when I had cast the spell.

I missed her and the scent of tortillas and Frankincense that followed her everywhere. Abuelita had told me over and over, "the demon came after you because you are special. The soul-less bastard thought at five years old, you would be easy prey."

Surviving the episode meant I had been destined to learn all her magic. I never felt special . . . I merely shrugged and went along for the ride. She had told me true magic was a combination of ancient spells and science. Hidden laws of the universe created this magic and used in the battle between light and darkness . . .

"True magic," she would say, "has the power to turn emptiness into pure light."

* * *

Abuelita secretly trained me the weekends my parents had to work. One Saturday morning, I anxiously waited for her to pick up me and my sis. Hours went by and no one came. This struck me as bizarre because she never was late. My moms itched with irritation because she needed someone to open up her shop. A bad feeling churned in my stomach. Finally, the phone rang. Abuelita's neighbor, Mrs. Chico, called screaming in hysterics. She had said that my abuelita had not met her for their 5am walk and went to check on her. Mrs. Chico found her dead. The unexpected death crushed all of us, especially Dad. My parents never explained how she died. My sis and I were allowed one day to help clean up the tiny apartment, where I found her vintage coin collection and a secret notebook of spells. This I kept for myself.

* * *

The hydraulic hiss when the bus stopped jarred me from my flashback. Chuy and I sighed . . . releasing our tension. Assisted by the teen, super-mom climbed onto the bus. Finally, our turn arrived. Three big steps taunted us.

"One —" I counted, praying Chuy had more guts than me. I could see stress in her posture, and fierce focus.

"Two —"

On three I shoved with all I had, and Chuy already inside pulled and pulled.

No! Epic fail. The suitcase might as well have been a boulder—Chuy and I puny lice.

"Excuse me," said the tall priest, "but can I be of some service?" Cool and calm, that voice, like some late-night radio deejay.

I assessed his skinny frame. *Hmmm . . . gonna need more than spiritual mojo here.*

Chuy beamed her thrilling smile. "Oh, please— *any* help would be appreciated."

"My pleasure."

The priest reached and gripped the suitcase, tendons and blue veins bulging in his hands.

With swift economy of movement, he plopped it onto the first step and glanced up at Chuy. "This is one heavy suitcase. What's inside?"

Chuy's eyes bulged; mouth frozen into an O large enough to swallow a sprinkled donut. "I . . . I . . . I—have a Paleolithic rock collection I'm donating to the museum."

The priest smiled . . . no—smirked.

"Liar, liar, *pants* on fire."

That once-soothing tone now became deep and menacing. *What the—bleep?!*

He leaned toward Chuy and whispered. Still and solemn, she blanked—blood threaded from her nose.

Terror blasted through me—and rage. "Chuy!"

The priest raised the suitcase and I could see his spindly wrist blackened with char.

He grunted like a drowning dog, clawed at his throat and whipped the clerical collar into my face.

His smug smirk revealed teeth pointy and long, as if filed. "Did you *miss* me, boooy?"

A warm stream of urine—*zooswosh*—ran down my pant leg. The demonic imposter zipped along the street and leaped onto a warehouse.

Nightmarish panic surged through me—his/its limbs twisted, as I watched, into spidery members. I couldn't even scream.

Chuy, paralyzed, stood waxy with blood streaming from her nose and striping her chin red. When I picked out the ashy imprint of a claw branding her forearm, I sickened and explosively vomited.

* * *

Sour stomach aching, and soaked by my own pee, I struggled with any sane response to police questioning (really more like interrogation).

Last thing I wanted was to sound more bonkers than a toothless cat trying to play the harmonica with its butt, and end up getting tased! What was I supposed to say? "Well, officer, this demon that almost ate me as a five-year-old came back to steal our suitcase. Yep — that's what I said. *Demon*. Did I mention we stuffed a dead dog into the luggage?"

Blurting out any of that probably would earn me a ticket to the nut house. Lunar's Looney Bin.

"If I'm following," said the officer, "the thief was disguised as a priest?"

"Yes."

"Were there expensive possessions inside the suitcase?"

"Uhm . . . uh — yes — no . . . I — dunno."

The reek of pee and vomit loitered in the air, and the police officer made obvious efforts to hide his disgust. "You've been through quite an ordeal. Stay calm, we're contacting your parents."

Gruff paramedics, impatient and exhausted-looking, scooped Chuy onto a shiny wheeled gurney. She bore that terrible empty gaze seen on newsflash trauma victims. Dried blood crusted her nostrils and lips.

I sat in the cordoned-off bus as police questioned witnesses and stumped around for clues. Why had that bleeping thing come back? What the bleep did it *want*?

The police zeroed in on the formerly super-mom-assisting teen. I scooched over to eavesdrop.

No mention of the evil thing climbing over a building.

Had no other witnessed the horrifying thing?

My hand bumped and knocked over someone's briefcase.

It popped open. Inside sat a brown paper bag and a tape recorder.

Without thinking I snagged both — scanned to see if anyone noticed. Here was the Bible the demon had held. I grabbed that too. I didn't want it, but my hands took control. Even though my brain shouted *Stop!* my fingers already flipped pages. Notably missing was a solid chunk of text, torn — no, chewed — out. Between jagged teeth marks, partly shredded and missing pages, lay blotches of some grey-black gunk. A sudden sulphury odor like burning matches and rot hit me. At once that unearthly voice demon-drilled my skull. *"Did you* miss *me, boooooy?*" Five-years-old again, I felt its burning grip on my arm and thrashed to escape.

The world got yanked out from under me. Then blackness. Then nothing.

* * *

I woke in a hospital bed. Moms perched beside me, caressed my pale hair. Little sis napped on a compact sofa in one corner.

Ten feet from me, my aunt and uncle stood over bed #2, where Chuy laid. Clear plastic IV lines snaked from her arms and climbed steel poles tipped with pinging white boxes winking green, red, and amber.

" . . . . Ma? . . . "

"*Mijo*—you're awake."

" . . . and Chuy?"

"She is going to be fine. They are just running a few more tests on her."

I tried pushing into a sitting position, but no dice. My arm muscles had no juice, no energy at all.

Seeing this, Moms swallowed hard. "Re*lax*, Nelio. You guys are safe now."

* * *

The next day, after some serious convincing, my moms agreed to let me stay with my aunt and uncle for a few days to help look after Chuy.

"Promise me," Moms said, "you will not take *one step* outside that house."

I agreed. Honestly, I padded carefully into Chuy's room.

Chuy's skin shone pallid and drawn, body flinching at any sound. She almost slapped me for farting. There we sat, like two restless zombies. I waited for Chuy to take out her journal, write down all the main events of the day and—as always—begin analyzing them. Instead, she clutched her Einstein teddy bear and quivered under her favorite blanket.

"Chuy, are we going to talk about what happened, or what?"

Impatient, I crossed my arms.

Chuy shot me a glance, gazed at her bandages, and down at the floor. Down, down, and down. "Myself . . . I don't think I can manage . . . what happened is . . . beyond reason and logic. Beyond critical thinking. A cataclysmic *nightmare*. I feel, well, torn from reality now—even from myself."

"God. What did it *say* to you?"

"I don't remember words, only its voice and . . . *images*. The sound came from a throat made of the universe's filthiest scabs. It felt eons old. Cut pictures into my soul of prehistoric darkness . . . the void seething within the first black hole howling and hungering to eat all light in existence. It was

something . . . something I'll never unsee, or forget —
"

"I know how you feel."

"Oh, Lunelio — I doubt that very much."

Pulling back my left shirt sleeve, I stooped and held my scarred arm beside Chuy's bandaged own.

Her eyes widened. "Ohh. Oh my God. . . it looks just like *mine* — do you think — "

"I don't think, I know."

"So that incident when you were little — it really *was* some demonic force."

"Yes. And now it's back."

"I'm so sorry. I never believed you or abuelita."

"It's okay, that doesn't matter now. We just need to work together and figure out why that evil bleep took Pebbles, we — "

"The *key*."

"Of course. And maybe that's why the Nacho Man ditched the dog with you and left town."

"No, Lunelio, I don't think he was ditching the dog. I think he tried *hiding* her."

"Either way, that dude sucks."

"Maybe now that it has what it wants, it will leave us alone."

Knots coiled like snakes in my belly. "I think I'm still on its dinner menu." Finally, Chuy stood. "That could be true."

Before her mirror, she ran a finger over cheekbones, lips, and carefully squeezed her nose. I could see, literally, life rekindling in her eyes and face.

"Hey, almost forgot — I found clues." I placed the tape recorder and paper bag on her bed. The Bible must have been taken by the police after I fainted.

Chuy dug into her closet and geared us up with blue examination gloves, face-protection masks, and lab coats. My hand trembled cradling the recorder. "If it's a creepy demon voice, I'm gonna pee myself again."

"Lunelcito, that would make two of us."

Tension ticked in that quiet room, and we both swallowed when I pressed Play.

[Tape hiss for several seconds, and a sudden moan. A voice choked with anguish and despair]:

"Please — please end this...I cannot bear any more. I . . . ah god . . ."

"Pathetic human, it ends when I decide it ends! Hehehehahahaha."[Prolonged screaming, as if under physical torture]

"Just . . . just kill *me already repugnant demon. I can't even . . . NOOO!"*

[More crying out, higher-pitched this time]

"I've had enough *of you, mortal peon. Your existence is beyond annoying me."*

"Aaaaaaaaaaaaaaah!"

The voice bellowed one last time.

Then came the sound of something organic being torn . . .liquid spattering. Hollow silence, then, disrupted by dripping . . . then white noise/tape hiss. An abrupt growl came, guttural . . . what could only be some large beast (dog, tiger, bear, unknown creature?) fiercely masticating. Whatever it might be invaded the safe silent space of Chuy's room. The sound grew louder. Static popping, electric snapping, and grunts of apparent enjoyment. My fizzing imagination, unfortunately, envisioned a char-black monstrosity devouring its victim.

Man! What came next . . . well, I'll call it what it struck me as being: cackling, wicked and throaty. Icy fingers traced my spine, and I got a vision of cold, creeping horror. Snapping sounds, like branches . . . and a single word screamed in my brain—*bones.* *"Hehehehaha. Are you enjoying this as much as I? If you're listening, you have something that belongs to me. Give me the bleeping dog or suffer the same agonizing fate."*

If some abomination could crawl from a crack between worlds, from eternal nothingness, it would sound like what we heard.

"Turn it off," Chuy whispered, "stop it."

Paralyzed with fright and revulsion, I couldn't move, so she switched off the recorder. "Lunelio, that voice . . . *pleading* . . . begging for mercy . . . I think I recognize it."

"Chuy, I'm going to spend the rest of my life trying to erase from my mind what we just heard . . ."

"Yeah, well I'm done sleeping for the rest of my life."

"Sleeping is over-rated Chu-ster. Pardon me while I go to the bathroom and change my underwear."

I stood and moved clumsily, legs cold from adrenaline rush. In the bathroom, I splashed my face with warm water and looked at my hair. Had it turned even whiter?

Stepping back into the room, I found Chuy staring at the brown paper bag.

"Wait," I blurted, "is it just me or is the bag moving."

"Lunelio, the bag is *definitely* moving."

"I already lost my hair-color and now will probably have to start wearing diapers again. Let's toss the bleepin' thing in the garbage and call it a day."

Chuy gazed at me as if I'd grown a second head. "*What*? You know we can't do that."

"What the hell, can things really get much worse?"

"I pray not."

She plucked the paper bag and opened it.

"Ugh! That reeking rot again! Gag me . . ."

Inside, maggots writhed like boiling water as they feasted on a hunk of rotting meat.

Under the dead flesh glistened a photo of Chuy, my abuelita, and myself holding hands in a park four years ago. I pinched out the photo, and Chuy dashed to the bathroom and flushed the maggoty meat down the toilet. My eyes fixated on the picture's flipside, where something had scrawled a message using what resembled dried blood — or something: *I'VE COME BACK FOR YOU BOOOOY.*

* * *

A Bucket of Ice Water

I shambled through the hallway, everything foggy as if some weird filter obscured my eyesight. Out of school for a week, sleep-deprivation pulled at my eyelids and made me punchy. My crew surrounded me.

"*Dude-dude-dude-duuude,*" buzzed Twitch, "where have yuh been?"

"Bro-mano," Math said, "we were deeply concerned."

Hollywood chimed in, "Boss, I thought you were dead."

Math slapped him on the shoulder. "Hollywood, stop speaking nonsense."

My chance now. "I'm sorry, bro-manos. I . . . I . . ."

"Lunar, spit it out already. What the heck balls happened to you?"

I took a deep breath. "It's back . . ."

"*It?*" said Twitch.

* * *

We sat down in the cafeteria, and I told them everything. The three of them stared at me as if a monkey flung poo from my head.

"Holy shiitake!" said Hollywood.

"Lunar, that's quite a dreadful predicament," said Math. "You and Chuy are going to need our help."

I gave a stoic nod. "And a church full of miracles."

"I'll do anything for Chuy," blurted Twitch. "She's my future wife."

He doodled stick-figures—bride and groom—on his notebook.

The rest of us shook our heads at his impossible fantasy.

I yanked on my hair. White fibers rained onto my shoulders. Great, now I had started to go bald. So much stress. I could think of nothing but how my life would end as demon tacos.

"*Ahem.*"

Math cleared his throat, fingers tapping nervously on the table. Something was up. "Lunar, I know there's an ocean of worry in your mind, but I must update you—"

"Dude," Twitch cut in, "I hope you brought your dancing shoes."

I didn't like the sound of *that*! "What?"

"Lunar, you've been gone since last week," Math "helpfully" reminded, "and it seems none of our messages reached you."

"*And?*"

"Well, today is your dance duel with Bola."

"Oh my bleep, I forgot that ever was a thing."

I banged my head against the table. "*Why* is this happening to me?"

"Lunar, look at the bright side, dude," Twitch bright-sided me. "If Bola eats you, then you won't have to worry about the demon anymore."

Math squinted. "Twitch, we've been through this, rub two brain cells together before speaking."

"Sometimes the right path is not the easiest one," said Hollywood."

"Aw crap," I said, "that's just another one of your stupid movie quotes."

He simply nodded, shrugged it off.

"Lunelio, why are banging your head?"

Immediately I stopped the self-torment. "Hey...Viorica. Cuz...life is so awesome."

"Awesome? Dude, your life is a living nightmmm—"

Math palmed Twitch's mouth.

Undaunted, Viorica crossed her arms. "Where have you been? I've been worried."

"You've been worried...about *me*—really?"

"Yes, really."

"Thanks, I guess?"

"We will give you two some privacy." Leave it to Math, our diplomat.

"Lunar and Viorica sitting in a tree, k-i-s-s—"

Promptly Hollywood and Math wheeled away Twitch, leaving behind an awkward silence. Viorica stood peering at me. "Can I sit down?"

"Of course."

"What's wrong?"

"I'm just tired…"

Leaning closer, she appraised my eyes. "You're not telling me the truth."

"Umm…this dance-off duel thingy…it's got me nervous."

"No. There's something else. I see it in your eyes."

"Viorica…you wouldn't believe me."

Abruptly she grabbed my hand, flipped it, and locked her gaze onto my palm. Electricity zinged through my pores—my internal temp heated up.

"Hands reveal secrets about one's destiny, Lunelio."

"Great. Am I destined to die young?"

"Please tell me what happened to you."

So I did.

* * *

After, I could see worry in Viorica's soulful eyes. She brushed a finger over my scarred arm.

"So, you believe me?"

"Yes," she said, and winced. "There's something I need to tell you."

"Okay." Her tone stirred nervous bubbles in my belly.

"I have to—"

BOOM. The lockers rattled as if from a bomb blast. The floor shook.

"LAAAAAMELIO!"

Viorica's mouth dropped open—I gripped her hand and we dashed out of there.

* * *

"Come out, come out, wherever you are lame-elio."

Another terrifying roar ruffled the hair of everyone in the hallway.

I turned to face Bola, guided Viorica safely behind me.

Bola's footfalls detonated, shaking windows in their frames and opening the crowd like a homicidal Moses parting the Red Sea. His shadow, like activated charcoal, sucked out the light.

"Rumor was you ditched town in a diaper somethin. After today you'll wish you had."

His breath-blast reeked of fast food left rotting under a car seat.

My eyes watered. Nose hairs withered and died. Behind me, passed-out bodies slapped to the floor.

"Me and you, dance with death behind El Desmadre Taqueria after school. Don't chicken out or somethin, I know where you live."

Behind him, Weasel laughed. "I hope you brought something nice to be buried in. Heedeedeedehehe." Beside Bola appeared his minion, Gee Slice.

This surprised me. Gee Slice, caught bringing a weapon to school, was rumored to have been expelled and sentenced to life. Gossip claimed the police had found bodies under his bed.

"Yo yo yo, look at the shmoe. Don't be chicken and avoid yo lickin. Cuz no matter what, yo life-clock will be runnin outta tickin." Gee Slice's lankness, baggy eyes, oversized gym shoes, and unclean teeth revolted me — put fire in my eyes. I opened my mouth to slam him, but Twitch beat me to the punch.

"Ffffirst off greasy meatball, buy some toothpaste, mouthwash, and breath mints. Place all three in a blender with holy water. Blend, drink, and bathe in that for the rest of your life. Bola's nostrils flared; eyes glowed with murder. One of those gaping nose-holes could swallow Twitch!

"That's *enough*, Bola," said Viorica.

That powerful voice surprised me, silenced the chattering crowd. Bola retreated one step, wincing and snarling. "It's time for you and your little friends to go and —"

"Prepare for a duel," Math cut in, "to see who's got the fuel for the most dab-tastic moves and grooves." This ignited a spark in the crowd, and they blazed into a chant:

"*DANCE DUEL, DANCE DUEL, DANCE DUEL, DANCE —*" Beneath the cheers Bola cussed, gave me the universal I'm-gonna-slaughter-you gesture — slicing his throat with a finger. The bully sneered at the crew and they backed off.

Math's sudden shout hooked Gee Slice's rare attention. "Gee Slice, today will be the day you learn how to rhyme and flow from a fearless hero. Your words are meek and your mind is weak. A lesson from Math is what you need. Some knowledge, your inferior brain, I will feed."

Gee Slice's mouth yawned open, but no comeback came. He gave Math the ol' finger (indicating Math was #1, right?). We exploded into laughter.

"Dude, you're so *clueless*," Twitch pointed out.

Teachers shouted, waved us out like herded cattle. No choice but to head off to our various classes.

* * *

The school bell rang. Time for me to face the music. I rushed to meet my crew. Two hands yanked me toward the stairs, and I thrilled to see they were attached to Viorica. "Lunelio, don't go through with this duel."

"I have to."

"Lunelio, hurt people, hurt people."

"Huh? What're you talking about? There's no turning back for me now."

"There are bigger things at stake."

"You don't think I know that? After I'm down with this meathead, I have to find a way to stop that demon from using my bones for toothpicks."

"Lunelio, there are things you don't know."

"Like what?"

"There's no time to explain. I have to leave."

"Leave? You're not going to the duel?"

"No, and you shouldn't either." Those words really ice-bucketed me. "Where are you going?"

"I can't tell you."

"Why not?"

"I…"

"What, are your parents leaving town?"

"Something like that."

"When are you coming back?"

"I don't know…if I will."

"Are you *serious*? —"

"Lunelio, I'm sorry."

"Holy bleep, *now* you tell me this. I thought you cared about me. I thought we were friends."

"We are and I *do*."

"I thought we could've, ya know, maybe been *more* than friends."

She paused, but not long. "I'm sorry, Lunelio. I don't have a choice."

"*Ha*. What a joke. I thought you were special — that I meant something to you."

"Lunelio —"

"*No*, Viorica, I don't wanna hear any more of your lies. You're a lying, phony jerk."

At that moment her eyes seemed to glow with soft purple fire. A tear dropped, traced her cheek and dotted the floor. I turned away.

"Lunelio," she began to whisper. Her words slipped underneath my ears. Was she praying? Abruptly she reached and hugged me from behind, pressed something into my hand.

"I'm leaving now."

"Good, go," I said. "Don't want you here anyway."

I maintained the cold shoulder, but, with each of her fading footsteps my world seemed to crumble. Her sweet jasmine aroma lingered. I turned around, but Viorica was gone.

A Dance-Off or A Funeral

The wind whooshed behind El Desmadre restaurant. Only the four of us stood there, and my nerves jangled along with my legs. I couldn't think straight, or even connect thoughts.

The restaurant sighed a spicy mist of garlicky fried food and hot chile oil. I imagined death-row inmates receiving their last meal.

Ouch.

A sharp sting to my palm. I realized — or recalled — why I'd clenched my hand.

Opening it revealed a shiny charm inscribed *P.V.*

What could they stand for? My heart ached. I should have known Viorica would end up breaking it like cold china. What had I been thinking? A girl like that could *never* like a white-haired freak like me. Hollywood observed my troubled face, patted my shoulder. "Before the victory, there is always pain."

Easy for *him* to say — his heart hadn't been splintered.

Twitch ignored us. "Your audience is arriving, woot-woot."

Kids held signs: *Go Lunelio* and *Show Bola Whose Got Bolas.* Math nodded confidently. I stretched, always good for snuffing tension.

Across the alley appeared a bloated shadow and a rain cloud with lesser shadows that brought a storm of despicable laughter.

Cracks veined my confidence. Would it crumble? "Lunar Eclipse, know that you will unleash righteous justice with your mad skills," Math jump-started my flat-lining spirit. And in this duel, you will leave this fool in shame while you triumph in fame."

"Heedeedeedeehehe," Weasel gushed. "I hope you're ready for a science lesson on what worms do to your flesh once you're *dead*." Bola's grim sneer chilled my bones. My bravery ran and hid behind the sweat on my buttock.

Twitch, wired, swung his legs like nun-chucks. "Dude, shut your trap before I beat you with my legs." Faking bravery, I glared at Bola. He cracked his knuckles, Weasel shook a bucket of popcorn, and Gee Slice carved a tiny coffin with my name on it. The crew surrounded me and we went over my game plan.

BAM. BAM. BAM.

Our necks craned over to Bola punching a brick wall with his bare fists. With each Bola-slam, cement dust rained over him and his crew. Math and Hollywood grabbed me before I fell to my knees.

"Let's start the duel already or somethin. My fists are hungry."

Math faced me, lowered his sunglasses, and for the first time in our friendship's history revealed his eyeballs. They looked like pale gray marbles floating in a milky mist.

"Control your emotions. Once you defeat the beast you'll be a hero and his reputation will be less than zero."

I glared back dumbfounded as he put his shades back on.

"A true hero isn't measured by the size of his strength," said Hollywood, "but by the strength of his heart."

"Dude, you got this. Just don't pee yourself," said Twitch.

I regarded my bro-migos, legs going soft like jelly, and got suddenly brain-jacked by a memory: my former dancing-coach, a Scotsman named Angus Carmichael McPherson. In his studio after hours of practice, I marinated in sweat, muscles screaming and limbs turning into mush. Coach's bald pink head gleamed; ripped biceps threatened to burst his sleeves. A tattooed dumbbell on one arm bore a bold script: *No pain, no gain*

In full Scots brogue, Coach shouted, "Listen boy-o, trrrue heroes arrre not blind to fearrr. They strrraight feel it. With that fearrr scrrreamin in theirrr face, a hero acts anyway. It's yourrr choice. On one end is the safe and regrrretful life of a cowarrrd. On the otherrr, is the dangerrrous and empowerrring life of a hero."

Thwack. Twitch's slimy hand smacked my face. "Wakey-wakey, dude."

A lion's courage roared inside me. "You guys are right. I can do this."

Math waved his cane, commanded the buzzing mob into a hush, and raised a microphone. At a thumbs-up, Twitch activated speakers lashed to the wheelchair's back. "All right, all right. Things 'bout to get spicier than kimchee. For this dance-off, I will be your referee."

The crowd roared. Gee Slice sneered at Math. "Who died and made *you* —"

Luis Rodriguez

"Twitch," interrupted Math, "clear a dance area for our contenders."

"Outta the way, yuh lumps." Twitch zigzagged a path through the crowd.

Hollywood and I performed our secret handshake.

"May the force be with you," he said.

I nodded and advanced toward the dirt patch beside the alley — our dance-battle "stage."

Math blared, "Arrrre you ready for the dance battle of a lifetime?"

The crowd yelled as one.

My time to shine. "*Math* — drop me a beat."

"I move like uh ghost and spit out rhymes as tasty as peanut butter on toast. Puh tis, puh-puh-puh tis. Puh tis, puh-puh-puh tis…" The rhyme rolled into an energetic beatbox.

"You ready lame-elio?" Bola shouted.

"Yeah, I am, you laboratory experiment gone wrong. I plan to give you a lesson in standing-up-to-bullies 101."

Veins like angry worms writhed under his leathery forehead. "AAARRRGH! You gonna *pay* for that or somethin."

I stepped over to the cardboard box Twitch left for me, quickly unfolded it while moving robot-style. I shrank myself into a ball, and Math paused the beat. The crowd waited.

"Ahhhhh yeah. I gotta a hot note, now let me clear my throat. BaRrrrrrrrrrrrrrrrr…"

BOOM.

Math exploded an earth-rocking beat. This sonic blast vibrated every cell in my body, and I sustained robot-style, mechanically hatched from my ball form. Lifted my arms, turned my shoulders, and moved my body in sync with Math's beat—feet flipped into a reverse moon-walk, and I twisted into a 360-spin ending with an aggressive finger-point at Bola.

The crowd cheered!

Bola snorted at me, tromped to the dance floor, grimaced at the crowd and halted. "Gee Slice, gimme uh beat so I can eat down this *chump*."

Rudely Gee Slice snatched the microphone from Math.

"My name is G slice,

Step to me, prepare to get sliced.

No ladies I don't have lice, but I am damn nice.

Don't make me say it twice.

Now watch my man Bola and his dope moves

the eyes may confuse, but I know the crowd won't refuse.

Bola, roll the dice and make this bum lame-elio pay the price."

Immediately Bola jumped up and down, thrusting his arms in the air like a bloated Franken-cheerleader while shaking his waist side to side. He then started dabbing for what seemed like hours. The bully looked to be stuck on repeat smelling his armpits. Next, Bola peeled off his shirt, swung it in the air, slid it between his legs — and threw it to me!

Time stopped. The crowd froze.

A mosquito stuck to Weasel's head. Twitch drooled from a crazed smile. Above me, midair, hovered the huge shirt — sweat-stained pits, and a reek of fast-food farts. I could tell it hungered to smother me to death.

Time resumed, and I ran for my life.

Splat. The shirt draped my head and face, coated me in Bola's thick body-gravy. "Noooooooooooooooooooooooooo!" Bola's sweat oozed down my neck. I fell to my knees and choked. "Oh my bleep, it's in my *mouth.*"

I heard people gasping and three jerks cackling.

Twitch said, "Get a hold of yourself dude."

"Damn-it, Lunar," raved Hollywood, "there is no crying in a dance battle."

WHOOOSH.

Math blasted me with a water hose — now that frozen water baptism had me reborn! I catapulted out of the stream of H2O and faked a backward fall. Hitting ground, I dropped into a reverse worm all the way to the dance floor.

Math restarted his beatbox:

"G slice your rhymes are more tragic,
then a legless clown tryin to do magic.
I may be blind, but unlike you I have mad-vision.

You don't stand a chance against my verbal collision.

Ladies and gentlemen, behold, the king of the dance.

Before your eyes, he is taking an honorable stance,

Bola just took on a foolish mission impossible.

Defeating my man, even Nostradamus knows is implausible."

The crowd rumbled.

I craned myself into a handstand, dropped my legs two inches from the ground. The crowd sputtered *oooo* and *oooh*. I contorted into an L-shape, smiled at Bola and his crew. I spun, twirled my legs and body. Back on my feet, I returned to robot-mode and moonwalked to Bola.

I stopped directly before him and raised his crusty shirt. Bola gazed at what I'd written on it while spinning like an acrobat: *You just got served.*

The crowd rubbed its eyes and supernovaed with cheers.

"Lunelio! Lunelio! Lunelio!"

Bola's face imploded, flashed slaughterhouse red. I made a 180-degree spin and dashed for a brick wall as if in collision. The crowd watched in shock.

"Reerrer." Math's beat-box scratched to a halt.

A moment before crashing into it, I leaped, took three running steps on the wall, and backflipped — *Thud.* I landed safely, and a mist of silence hung in the air. The audience went ballistic. *"Yaaaaaaay."*

I watched Bola's chest expand and contract. "*RRRRRAUGH!*" Dashing to the back of the alley, he snatched a Dumpster, raised it over his head like steroid-infused Donkey Kong. In the middle of the violent drama something fell from Bola's pocket with a *clink* – a copper locket with an attached chain. Bola plucked it from the ground and rabidly growled. Drooling, he stomped toward me.

The mob dispersed like panicked cockroaches.

Bola launched the Dumpster. Paralyzed, I could see my gravestone: *Death by dumpster, how pathetic.* I held out my arms in a desperate attempt to stop my life from ending, chomping my lip as I clinically observed the Dumpster's 100 mph roll toward me. My eyes slammed shut, and sharp flaming pain ate into my leg as if a fire leech tunneled there. *Kkkrrrrsshhkeeesh.*

I opened my eyes.

How could I still be breathing? And why was I not drowning in agony with my new pancake body? My eyes bulged — what the bleep? The iron trash-box stopped an inch in front of me. I saw a splotch of blood over the pocket of my jeans. My hand crawled inside and found Viorica's charm embedded in my leg meat.

"The Dance-off us over, Bola bellowed like a beast and fired more Dumpsters into the air.

His ominous roars rattled our hearts and garbage rained over us. Everyone scrammed, including his entourage. My bro-manos and I grabbed our things and fled as if evading WWIII. We cut through a park and paused for a breather. Kids appeared and came to shake my hand — broke into chanting my name! What a buzz! Something I only experienced in my looniest dreams. At that moment, a throng of people, including my crew, snatched me and lifted me into the air — tossed me up and cheered as if I had just scored the winning goal in the World Cup.

I thought about Viorica and my triumph melted into emptiness . . .

Her words had been so confusing, so secretive. Questions buzzed in my mind like mosquitoes. I then envisioned — yeesh! — Bola's face. I had seen his eyes full of tears, cheeks blood-red, face scrunched with pain. I stood up to him, won the battle, and miraculously survived his Dumpster attack. Why wasn't a hero's fire burning in my belly? Like a splinter, I pinched Viorica's charm from my leg. I wiped it clean and cupped it in my hand. The crew surrounded me with proud smiles. My face felt heavy and my heart fractured. "Lunar, you wear the champion's crown yet all we see is a frown?" said Math.

I sighed. "Why are girls so confusing?"

Twitch shrugged, gnawed a fingernail. "C'mon dude, no one gets girls. They are as confusing to us as a Rubik's Cube is to a gerbil."

Math lay a sympathetic hand on my shoulder. "My compadre, men will never understand women.

That is one of the many laws of the universe. Same as atoms popping in and out of existence. Why does this happen? Where do they go? Where do they come from?"

"Huh? Math, what the bleepbomb.com are you talking about?"

"There are things we will never understand but must accept."

Oh bleep, it was getting late. If I didn't get home quick, my butt would taste chancla thrashings. We scurried off like squirrels in the middle of traffic.

The Letter

On my pillow sat a small box. I opened it. Immediately, scents of vanilla and wilderness filled my room. There rested inside a scroll, and my heart skipped a beat. I knew it was from Viorica. I ran downstairs.

"Ma, did someone come by to drop off a package?"

"No mijo, are you expecting something in the mail."

"Nah, just curious."

Moms' eyes peered suspiciously. I grinned, darted back to my room, and locked the door. I unrolled the scroll. The writing looked incredibly neat. The ink reminded me of those feather pens from the ancient times when men thought it cool to wear girly wigs. At the bottom of the box were two little-kid books. One about farts and the other a volume of Dr. Seuss. I chuckled and stood utterly confused.

* * *

Dear Lunelio,
You have been through a lot, I know. I still remember the little boy who bravely stood by his mother after the disappearance of your father. I have a dangerous journey I must embark on. It hurts me to keep you in the dark, but for now, it is best. If I make it back alive, I will explain

everything. What I must tell you now is that your abuelita had been part of a sacred tribe of shaman sorcerers. The tribe took in an orphan and your abuelita mothered her. The child grew up being trained and taught the secrets of true magic. As a young woman, she violated tribe sacred law and they banished her. This broke your abuelita's heart. The young woman tried to make amends to right her wrong. She died brutally in the process. The young woman left behind a baby. The baby became an orphan too. The baby grew up with a lot of suffering. Bullies tormented the child. He had no mother or father to love and guide him. This is why Bola has so much anger inside. The books I left for you were the crime Bola committed. His adopted abuelita can't afford to buy books and he practices reading to her at night. She is all he has, and she is very old. Soon, he will have no one again. The both of you share a special bond. You must find a way to come together.

Remember that your abuelita saw great power in you. Use the secrets she taught you. Keep my charm close to your heart, it will protect you. I will keep thoughts of you close to my heart. I hope to see you again one day.
XOXO,
P.V.

My fingers trembled; tears slid down my cheeks. How was any of this possible? How did she know about abuelita? Bola and I have a *special bond*? Why did she sign it P.V.? I couldn't wrap my brain around any of this. I put the letter back in the box and placed it in my safe. I leather-strung her charm, and wore it around my neck.

A Flashback and a Chanclaso
(aka Sandal Smack)

I walked into my pops' study and closed the door. In this place, my pops said he would find a solution whenever he fell into a problem. My moms kept family pictures throughout the room. She said it made her feel like he would know we were always thinking of him. Some moments my moms would throw a picture against the wall and glass would shatter into pieces. I would hear her cry out.

"Why did you have to leave? Why did you take that stupid mission? You knew it was dangerous."

My little sis and I would dash to her rescue and smother her with hugs until the tears passed. I quickly grew suspicious of my moms. I could tell she kept secrets about Pops. In fits of rage, I demanded she tell me.

"Was he kidnapped? A spy? Abducted by a UFO? Did someone *murder* him?"

My interrogation always ended the same way: moms sobbing, a picture frame crashing to the ground, and my little sister yelling, "You're making things worse."

There seemed to be secrets hiding all around me. Viorica's letter had been a grenade of black swans and secrets. Too many pieces I never imagined might exist. As my pops often did, I sat down, closed my eyes, and remained quiet. For the first few moments, a whole lot of nothing happened. Then blurry images appeared in the dark space of my mind. My abuelita's kitchen came into focus. I could hear the sizzling of food in a pan . . . smell the aroma of spices . . . see my abuelita rolling out homemade corn tortillas. I could even see five-year-old me before the dreadful demon had stolen my shiny black hair color.

"Your turn, mijito," said my abuelita.

Little-me stood on a stool and grabbed a glop of masa. I next formed the corn-dough into a ball, and placed the ball into an iron tortilla press. It came out shaped like a deflated balloon. I frowned while eyeing the stack of perfectly round tortillas abuelita had made.

"Mijito, be patient. Making tortilla takes practice. I've been practicing for 70 years."

"No way, people can live that long?"

Abuelita shook her head and looked like she considered breaking a chancla over mine. Then, from her garden-unit window came a fierce meow. A giant creature with glowing yellow eyes appeared. It looked like a cat, only much bigger and with the fangs of a beast. It lunged toward us and smashed into the window. Blood squirted from its forehead and spattered the glass. Little-me fell and screamed. *Booof! Booof! Booof!* The creature continued ramming the window. The frame broke and shards spat everywhere. My abuelita exploded into thundery shouts.

"Back, wretched demon, back!"

Each of her roars flickered the lights and shook the walls. Cement dust powdered us. The creature drew back several steps. Abuelita held up her hands. A blue glow charmed her palms, fire burned in her eyes. Little-me crawled into a safe nook.

"*Vil Tenebris Victa!*" hollered abuelita.

Blue lightning blazed from her hands and exploded into the darkness — my first glimpse of the intense power of true magic. The creature reappeared with a missing ear. It opened its snout and released an awful cackle. Little-me covered his ears. The creature began to choke. A pause . . . then the beast vomited hundreds of black widow spiders. The eight-legged assassins had lumpy bodies dotted with glowing red. Abuelita's voice roared again. "*Ignis De Dios!*" Blue fire shot from her hands, incinerated the spiders, and burned the creature's nose off. The wretched thing shrieked in agony and fled. Little-me trembled in one kitchen corner. Abuelita hobbled over and offered a wrinkled hand. "Mijito, it's *safe* now. You can come out."

Little-me could hear blood dripping from the broken basement window. Crawling across the floor, I felt something stab my knee. It was a locket. I pressed a small button and it opened. A young woman's pretty face looked back at me. My abuelita snatched it from my hand.

"That does not belong to you."

"Who is that?"

"Someone I used to—It is of no matter," she snapped.

Little-me lowered his head. "Okay."

She lifted me in her arms. "Mijo, the world is so heavy with secrets, I sometimes wonder if it might stumble off its axis. For you,

the ancient art of true magic can no longer remain one of those secrets. Your training begins now."

Abuelita cupped my almost five-year-old hands and whispered.

Tap-tap-tap. The knocking startled me awake. I looked at my hands. A blue flame appeared inside them and quickly vanished. If only Abuelita would have taught me more. I didn't feel prepared to fight off a hangry squirrel, much less a powerful demon. I rubbed my forehead. Tonight, I will begin studying her book of spells. Wait, that locket… It looked awfully similar to the one Bola had dropped. That lady's face—could it have been the same person? Viorica's letter started to sound less strange while making me feel stranger. Goosebumps rippled down my skin. What should I do now? Aha, I know—

Tap-tap-tap. "I can hear you talking to yourself."

"Iolani, go away, I'm busy."

"No, I have every right to be in papá's room just as you."

"Fine." No use arguing. My little sis could bug me for days straight. I opened the door.

"Why were you talking to yourself?"

"None of your business what I do."

"Lunelio, that's the first stage of going crazy. It only gets worse from here. Soon you'll be in an insane asylum . . . but don't feel too sad. I'll come visit you from time to time and bring fish food for you to feed your socks."

My little sis walked in a 9-year-old's shoes, but spoke as if 50. A hardcore bookworm, extremely nosy, and always bugging me at the worst moments.

"Hey little sis, I'm so glad I ran into you. I've been meaning to deliver a message. So, the adoption agency called and said they have a no-returns policy. Yeah, so moms has to keep you despite her tenth time sending in return papers. Oh wait, maybe that message was meant for *her*. Oh well, have a nice day."

Iolani's dark eyes examined me. She was unimpressed. "Looks like we just discovered being a comedian is not in your future. So, write down 'being funny' on the long list of things you're not good at."

I palmed her face. "Be gone, brat. Go read a book or something. I don't have time for you right now."

Iolani scowled and stuck out her tongue. "Why don't you start using some hair dye so that white fro on your head stops embarrassing me. All my friends think you're my grandfather."

No she didn't . . . My little sis knew making fun of my hair was off limits. Now she would have to pay the consequences. "Little girl, leave me alone. Otherwise, I will call for the thing that came for me at

5 years old. I will ask it to wait under the darkness of your bed, with its sharp claws, burnt black body, and blood-red eyes. You might think hiding under a blanket will save you. It won't. The demon will smell your fear and get hungrier. After a while, it will grow silent. You will think you're safe and begin to fall back asleep. This is exactly when the thing will grab your arm, pull you under the bed, and —"

"Lunelio, I said STOP."

Iolani slapped her ears closed attempting to un-hear my words and ran out of the room.

Had I gone too far? She would probably be in her bedroom curled up in a ball. I had better go apologize before — I glanced at the time — oh *bleep*. The day had melted into night. I needed to stop by Chuy's house. Ever since our run-in with that evil thing, Chuy hid from the outside world like a turtle in its shell. I ran out of the room. *SMACK.* Something hit me in the forehead and I crashed to the floor. A dark menacing figure stood over me armed with another chancla.

"Before I yell at you, are you okay?"

"I'm ok," I squealed.

Moms glared down. "Please get up."

She stared grimly.

"Lunelio Fernando Portillo, how dare you scare your little sister like that? You know she is sensitive and has an overactive imagination. Especially after your father's dea — disappearance. Do you remember the last time you scared her?"

I nodded.

"She could not sleep for a month, so *I* did not sleep for a month."

Every time I remembered, guilt burned in my belly. I could still picture her shaking and hugging her teddy. "Sorry ma, I have a lot on my mind and—"

"You're sorry? You're SORRY?" My moms' rage rose along with the shadow of a sandal over my face. But she took a breather. "Mijo, you know I love you, but you must learn to treat your little sister with care. You are her older brother. Now go apologize to her and be thankful I didn't use this second chancla."

"That's fair." I watched my moms lower the lethal sandal.

In her room, Iolani suffocated her teddy in a tight bear hug. I sat down and draped my arm around her. She quivered in fear.

"Leave me alone evil torturer." Her tiny voice peeped from behind the bear.

"I deserve that little sis. All I ask is you give me a chance to apologize."

Still, she hid behind the teddy.

"I have to be truthful with you. There is no demon. I made it up like a big jerk to scare you. I just got so angry . . . I couldn't help it."

"Then how did your hair turn all white?"

"Uhm . . . a birth defect."

"Wait, so will *my* hair turn white?"

"No." I had to think for a second. "It can only happen to the firstborn of the family."

Iolani looked at me and considered the information. "Is the Tooth Fairy real?"

I almost blabbed a *no* and stopped myself. "Oh, the Tooth Fairy . . . yeah, she is definitely real."

Tears streamed from her eyes. "I was *afraid* you would say that."

"Why?"

"Because then I know you are lying about the demon. Wherever there is good there is evil. There needs to be a balance to keep the fabric of space and time in harmony. I learned that from cousin Chuy."

"OMG, Iolani." I took a breath. "I'm sure cousin Chuy meant something different."

"Whatever, you weren't there." The teddy's seams threatened to tear from her harsh grip.

I stared at her with heavy eyes. I fell into another flashback of Iolani as a chubby baby swaddled and sleeping in her bassinet. Her eyes popped open. She looked at me and smiled. My heart melted (I won't admit that out loud). I swore then I would be her protector. Look at me now — I had to make this *right*. I sprinted to my room, opened the safe, and grabbed the only existing photo (*or so I thought*) of abuelita and her book of spells. I flipped pages, found what I needed, and wrote it down. I raced back to my little sis and kneeled to meet her eye-to-eye.

"Lunelio, whatever you're up to, it's weird."

I held my gaze. "Little sis, many many years ago, I made an oath to protect you. Today I have broken that oath a second time and I will dedicate the rest of my life to make it right. From the bottom of my soul, I'm sorry." I held up abuelita's picture.

"That's abuelita. Where did you *get* that?"

"Before she passed away, abuelita asked me to keep it safe."

"Lunelio, why don't we have more pictures of her?"

"Little sis, abuelita forbid pictures be taken of her."

"Why?"

"Because she thought pictures stole bits of your soul and could be used to hurt you if they got into the wrong hands."

"Not even a selfie?"

"Not even that. But she did give me this picture and asked me to keep it safe. She told me, after her death, it would protect us."

I held the picture, looked at the spell, and closed my eyes.

"Lunelio, what are you doing now?"

I then whispered the ancient words. "*Manus Dei Custodire.*" I felt electric ants crawl under my skin. The room's lights flickered.

"What's happening? You're freaking me out!"

"Done."

"What did you just do?"

"I cast a protection spell. Just keep abuelita's picture under your bed at night and nothing will harm you."

She dropped her bear and embraced me in a choke-hold.

"Holy smokes sis, take it easy. You must promise to keep her picture safe —"

"I will guard it with my life." Iolani gave the picture a kiss and placed it under her bed.

* * *

I walked back into my pops' office. Moms sat in his chair wearing his lucky suit jacket. Velvet black with burgundy trimmings, it boasted with style. The jacket had several small burnt singes. A small country at war showered bombs over cities full of innocent people. My dad said a bloody battle between the greedy and the poor roared with no end in sight. A school had just been attacked. Fire devoured the part of the building that had not been blown to bits. Kids were hanging out the windows screaming. My pops and his reporting crew were on scene. No police or firefighters were in sight.

"Pa, weren't you scared of dying?" I had asked him.

I remembered his anguished glare.

"Mijo, I could no longer watch the city burn down and doing nothing about it. I could not bear the fear of witnessing the fire eat the children alive."

Those words still gave me the chills. His team said it was a miracle. My pops sprinted into the school. Moments later, he burst out with three children as flames clung to his body. The building collapsed behind them. The day he arrived back home, my moms kissed and slapped him several times. I had never been so confused. My little sister thought it hilarious and rolled onto the floor laughing.

My moms hugged herself, stuck her nose inside the jacket, and took a deep breath. "The coat smells less of your father every time . . ." She fought back tears.

My eyes watered.

"I still talk to your father, mijo . . . at least once a day."

Yeah, *more like yell at him*, I thought to myself. The last time I spoke with him flashed in my mind.

"Pa, is there something wrong? Ma is crying. When are you coming home?"

From halfway across the world, his voice crackled on the poor phone connection.

"Mijo, I'm fine. Your mamá cares about me so she worries. I'll be home soon. This is my biggest story yet. Please be patient, and watch over your mamá and little sister."

I held back my tears. "Ma, can we save this talk for another time. I really need to see Chuy."

"Mijo, look at the time. It's already dark out."

"So?"

"So, tomorrow."

"Ma, I can't wait till —"

"Mijo, you don't talk to me anymore. I feel like you're keeping things from me. You're not sleeping much, you barely make time to eat, and a few weeks ago you almost gave me a heart attack when the policed phoned me that you were in the hospital."

I didn't know what to say. I couldn't tell my moms the truth. She wouldn't believe me. I could hear my pops voice and decided to fold.

"Ok, Ma." I didn't want her to stress out worse. "How about we watch a movie together?"

"I would like that, mijo. I'll get your sister, and you pick something out."

I faked a smile and she walked off. The silence in the room felt heavy. I thought about Viorica's letter, Bola, the demon, my abuelita, and my pops. Worry snakes coiled painfully in my stomach.

* * *

The Ambush

I had no choice, but to fake explosive diarrhea to get out of school. I almost lost my voice from grunting and screaming on the toilet. When Chuy opened the door, she looked relieved.

"Lunelcito, come in. Why aren't you at school?"

"Chu-ster, I'm on a quest and —"

"You need my help?"

"Exactly."

"Oh gosh, I had the most bizarre dream."

"Oh no, did that demon appear —"

"It actually wasn't a nightmare, Lunelio."

"Wait, you were able to fall asleep?" Shock and jealous tugged at my pore. "At night, I've had to sleep in my moms' room like a pathetic baby. And even then, I just stare at the ceiling for hours."

"Until last night, I've had nothing but nightmares of that . . . thing."

Chuy poured me some juice and began recapping her dream.

"I looked out the window and saw a beautiful forest. Then a girl appeared. She had long magenta hair and purple eyes. Her entire being glowed. I ran outside to her. A magnetic force felt to be pulling me. She told me the demon would return, we had little time, and that you would need me to help. Before I could ask her a million questions, she began to fade.

Before the girl disappeared, her last words were 'read the letter.' Then I woke up."

My eyes bulged and my heart winced in pain. Could it have been her? How? Who was she? Goose pimples rippled over my skin. I took out Viorica's letter and handed it to Chuy. "Cuz, I can't explain it, but I think the girl in your dream was the girl of my dreams."

"Huh?"

"Just read this letter."

After finishing, I explained to Chuy my tragic love story. She scratched her head and then began to draw formulas and diagrams on her nerdy dry-erase board.

"Lunelio, you're right. This is quite illogical. But then again so was that appalling monster. Either way, time is scarce. Let's go find this friend of yours."

"Whoa, Chuy, that guy is *not* my friend."

"If the words in that letter are true, he is like family." She half-smiled.

I cringed at the thought. Bola . . . *family?* "Whatever. Let's get this over with."

* * *

Chuy and I were coasting in her eco-mobile, aka solar-powered clown car. *She may be a little worn, but she does not pollute,* Chuy loved to say. She bought the car after three summers of working the following odd jobs: iguana-sitter (her last day she hid on the roof of the home after being attacked), a librarian's assistant (when Chuy's boss did not occupy herself sniffing books, she tried teaching cats to read Shakespeare), and a mortician's assistant (Chuy almost had a heart when a dead peep started moving his arms and legs. How could this be possible? The final fart had left his body.).

"So, Bola lives on the *east side* of town?" said Chuy.

"Yep."

"How do you know?"

"Chu-ster, when you live on the *east side* of town, *every*one knows."

Driving through Bola's neighbor*hood* we saw squirrels that looked as skinny as starving runway models. Scrawny pigeons attempted to poop on the car but instead farted dust. I saw a few kids in an alley kicking around a deflated soccer ball. We reached a stop sign. A chunky man pulled a rusty red wagon while his wife lay in it smoking a cigarette. Then a two-legged dog on a rickety wooden cart helped a blind cat cross the street. The cat held a walking stick. It tapped the car, turned, and gave us a toothless smile.

"Are you sure Bola will be at home?" said Chuy.

"No, but he hasn't been at school since he lost the dance duel. And if he's not at home, we can stop by the local jail and watch him do pushups."

Chuy rolled her eyes, and we continued forward. Every other house, boarded up with caved-in roofs, seem to cower with shame. We saw a family having a picnic in a depressing gray park, bald of grass, and one terminal tree coughing up dying leaves. We passed by rats and cockroaches with suitcases trying to hitch a ride out of the neighborhood.

"This place is so sad," I said.

"Lunelio, remember, it is more powerful to help others than feel sorry for them —"

"Stop the car Chuy, that's his house."

"Are you sure?"

"Just look at the huge door. It's wide enough to fit someone with an abnormally large head."

"Lunelio!"

* * *

A tiny old lady that had to be Bola's abuelita greeted Chuy, eyes owlish behind bifocals. I saw the abuelita break into tears and fall into Chuy's arms. Oh bleep, I instantly pictured a large coffin being dragged by a bulldozer. Relief and worry wrestled in my mind. Chuy jumped back in the car and set a box of musty books on my lap.

"Is he . . . dead?"

"*No.* Just missing."

My inside frosted. My pops also had *just* been missing. "What's in the boxes? Wait, is it body parts?"

"*Lunelio*, you really need to stop. They belong to your school."

"Chuy, I'm confused."

"His abuelita reads to Bola. He is barely literate…your friend that wrote the letter was right. He steals books because they are far below his grade level. He is scared someone might find out."

"Oh . . ." I thought about the note he had Weasel deliver me. Like cockroaches, guilt crawled under my skin.

"She hasn't seen him for two whole days."

"So he ran away."

"Lunelio, let's hope he hasn't gotten far—we have to find him."

* * *

As the dilapidated neighborhood passed outside the car windows, I couldn't help but think how often I wished Bola would disappear forever. Now we were one step away from creating a search party for him. I would put up signs on every block. *Missing: BOLA - A GIANT BULLY. If seen please call Lunar, the kid he almost ate.* We passed by a farmer's market with a labyrinth of food stands. Then, I spotted a large head.

"There he is." Chuy slammed on the breaks. "Go get him."

She pushed me out of the car.

With heavy legs, I trotted around a stand of toothy Venus Flytraps and passed a tamale lady. His melon head shuffled farther off. I began to speed up and tripped on a rock. I looked up, and over my head shone a machete. A stocky old man wrinkled like a raisin swung the giant knife. *Crack.* He smiled at me with drooping eyelids like flour dough and offered me coconut water. I cleaned the sweat from my forehead, handed him a dollar, and chugged it. I got back to my feet. Then a large shadow appeared over me — Bola.

He had his back to me. I ducked behind some pineapples. My heart raced. Damnit, why was I hiding from him? I peered in between the fruit and could see him clumping around suspiciously. I had to muster up the pistachios to face him.

From behind a pile of mangoes, I watched him walk to the tamale lady's stand. I took a deep breath and stood.

"Bo—"

His hand, as sneaky as a mosquito in the dark, snatched some tamales.

I slapped my mouth closed and dove behind piles of cilantro and parsley. Bola bumbled forward. I noticed the bottom of his jogging pants were tied with shoelaces. Jiggling at the bottom of them were stolen goods. *Swoop.* His sticky hands snagged up some aguacates. I watched them roll down his pants. I shook my head. Bola stole as stealthily as Pinocchio told lies.

"*Ahem.*"

I jerked, fell from my hiding place, and looked up with cilantro stuck in my hair. A beefy man, with a glass eye, and a caterpillar unibrow stood over me. I immediately became distracted by the tattoo of

Luis Rodriguez

circus clowns with x's over their eyes on his tree trunk forearm. He seemed to be pondering squishing me like a bug. I smiled nervously and grabbed the cilantro from my white fro.

"Sick tattoo, please don't kill me, and I'll take these."

His uni-brow scowled at me and he held out a hand larger than my head. I gave him the last dollar I had. He then pointed an angry finger signaling for me to leave or never see my next birthday.

"Good day, sir. By the way, you look tough enough to beat up a demon. Would you be up for the challenge?

He shook his head furiously and continued pointing his finger.

"I'll probably see you again in my nightmares." I sprinted off with my eyes bouncing left to right on guard for Bola. He was gone. Damnit, I totally screwed up. Then a heap of hullabaloo echoed from ahead. I slyly moved closer and saw several farmers around Bola. A viejita, the size and skin texture of a withered prune, smacked him with a chancla. Several other feisty old ladies grasped onto him.

"Thief—thief! Call the authorities. Have this sin vergüenza arrested," said one of the ladies.

They continued pinching and yelling at him. Then they grabbed their purses and circled Bola like a vicious merry-go-round. They began beating him like it was their job.

OMG, at any moment Bola would deliver each one of them to the grim reaper, one punch at a time. I moved to warn these old ladies that their lives were in jeopardy. Then tears, like a geyser, spewed from Bola's eye-holes. The ladies pulled out umbrellas as if out of a magician's hat, popped them open, and shielded themselves. He looked . . . pathetic and helpless. I felt a brush of air behind me. Then Chuy appeared like a super-hero and leaped in between Bola and the blood-thirsty elders.

"What do you think you're doing assaulting this child?"

"You call this ape-sized delinquent a child?" said the prune-sized abuelita.

"Name calling is not necessary," Chuy went on. "Furthermore, you have no right putting your hands on him."

Bola's volcanic sobbing simmered into a confused whimper.

"This so-called child is a thief. We have called the police and he is going to be arrested," said the abuelita.

Chuy squinted with contempt. "*Good.*"

My eyebrows curled in confusion. Chuy looked over and signaled me with her eyes. That's when I noticed a small wad of cash next to me. Wow, Chuy had acted ninja quick.

"When the police arrive, I will explain how my . . . cousin, is not a thief, but a victim of an elderly attack. Then we will see who is going to be arrested," she said.

The other abuelitas spoke up. "Excuse me young lady, are you calling us *liars*?"

"If the shoe fits…"

"How dare you!" said the prune abuelita.

"Excuse me, peeps. I've been waiting in line patiently for this drama to end so I can buy some . . ." I grabbed the first thing I saw. "Limes." I pointed to the money Chuy placed on the counter. "I saw that giant kid leave this cash here just before you started beating him."

The abuelitas turned to each other. Their cheeks flushed fire hydrant red.

"Here is a dollar for these limes. Please don't start beating me too." I pointed to my hair. "I have enough problems."

Chuy confidently crossed her arms. Bola lowered his head and stared at the floor. The abuelitas began pointing at each other accusingly.

"You said you saw him stealing."

"No, that was you."

"I did see him stealing."

"How can you see anything? You have cataracts."

Yes, Chuy's split-second plan had worked.

"Wait." Another abuelita, covered in scarfs like a mummified raisin, appeared out of nowhere. "Why does this hooligan have food stuffed in his pants?"

Bola shrugged, Chuy bit her lip, and everyone stared at his pants bulging with stolen goods.

"Uhmm . . . we — us kids do that. I always forget to bring grocery bags." I tucked my bottoms in my shoes and slid the limes and cilantro down my pants. "That's the cool way to carry stuff." I gave my best fake smile and felt my butt begin to sweat. I watched the ladies consider this.

Finally, the mummified abuelita said, "My grandchildren are as bizarre as sin. One eats with his feet. The other eats his mocos while wearing underwear on his head."

"My grandchild still has an imaginary friend and he is fifteen."

"My grandchild likes to sniff people's butts like a dog."

In between all the strange family confessions, Chuy grabbed Bola's hand, and we were off.

* * *

Awkwardness had been the soundtrack the entire ride to Bola's home. He answered all of Chuy's question with a NO, YES, or silence.

Chuy insisted we walk him to his front door. Bola finally spoke his first full sentence.

"Please don't tell my abue about me being a thief or nothin."

Chuy rubbed his massive shoulder. "We can keep a secret if *you* can."

Then came another eruption of water-works.

"I'm such a pathetic loser. . . yous shoulda let the cops pick me up . . ."

"Bolitas, you are not a loser," said Chuy. "Don't ever say that again."

My cuz put her arms around him. After soaking Chuy's shoulder with snot and tears, Bola calmed to a phlegmy sniffling.

"Lunelio, is there anything you would like to say to Bolitas?"

Only Chu-ster could nickname a rabid bully like that and survive. I ruffled my duck-nalga hair and held out my hand. "Bola . . . truce."

The sniffling stopped, and Bola kept silent. He left me hanging so I quickly hid my hand in my pocket.

"Bola, I don't want us to be enemies anymore. Maybe one day we could be allies." The words coming out of my mouth sounded so strange.

"What's an ally?"

"Uh, an ally? Its . . . uh . . ." I couldn't find the word.

"Friends, Bolitas. What Lunelio is trying to say, is you guys should be friends."
"Fffriends?"

I could see the oversized hamster in Bola's head moving.

"Why? Why do you want to be friends? Were suppose-ta be enemies or somethin."

"Why?" I asked.

"Cuz."

"Cuz why?"

"Just cuz . . . you and your friends are weirdos and I'm Bola."

"Well the way it works, doesn't work for me. It sucks."

"Whatever."

This conversation scuffed at a dead end. Then Viorica's letter and my flashback with abuelita lit up in my mind. "Bola, a long time ago my abuelita and your moms were . . . like family."

"What the bleep are you talking about? You don't know anything about my mom!"

"I know one thing, my abuelita had been like a mother to your moms. I also know you lost her and were left in an orphanage."

Bola's eye stretched to the top of his head and his mouth hung open. I had said too much. My brain said *run*, but MY legs stood as still as a gravestone. My eyes shifted left to right planning an escape route for Chuy and I.

"I . . . I . . . You don't . . . don't know . . . what you're talking about. I was never a loser orphan and stop telling lies about mom and your stupid abuelita."

"Bolitas, we are trying to help you."

"I don't want your loser help or nothin. Leave me alone." *WHAM.* His front door slammed, and the tiny home trembled.

* * *

(A NIGHTMARE)

My vision blurred as if surrounded by fog and my eyelids weighed 50 lbs. The moment they closed I heard a creak in the wood floor. I jumped out of bed, and forced myself to look underneath. What did I find? A sweaty me drowning in fear, no demon. With my lights on and door open, I still couldn't trust sleep. I was a mess. With my tail between my legs, I walked to my moms' room *again* and plopped down on the floor with my pillow. My drowsy eyes stared at the bedroom ceiling as I listened to moms' snore. Normally, this would go on for hours. But tonight, my body had enough. Darkness swallowed me and I drifted off to sleep.

Screaming jarred me awake. Bitter cold had invaded, and I walked in bare feet. My breath steamed.

The moon glared deep blood-red. Hunter's Moon.

I walked through a neighborhood strangely familiar. Where was I?

I heard the screaming again, but this time it grew louder. I looked and saw abuelita's home—ran toward it.

I could see two silhouettes in the window. The screaming grew louder, daggered my ears.

As I got closer to her apartment the cement turned to liquid. With each step, my feet sank.

121

Violent crashing echoed in the little apartment. I stared and watched blood spray over her curtains. Then blue electricity exploded—spraying the curtains with black ooze. The shrill of a creature shook the whole building. "Abuelita!" I screamed as I sank knee deep in cement.

Her door taunted me, now only a few feet from my grasp as I fought to trudge forward. *Crrrsssh.* Something smashed into the front window. I saw her curly salt-and-pepper hair and more blood. She screamed and more blue electricity lit up the room. I could hear the awful sounds of breaking bones and evil cackling. After what felt like a torturous century, I finally grabbed the doorknob and fell inside her living room.

Shadows and laughter lurked in each dark corner.

Blood spattered the walls.

A black shadow moved, and there she laid.

Still and silent, gashes covered Abuelita's body. Legs torn and hair caked with blood. Like a velvet rug, a pool of red circled her. It coated my naked feet like blood-socks. Then I heard more maniacal laughter. A dark shadow appeared and lifted abuelita off the ground. Her lifeless body jerked convulsively. As if from an endless bowl of blood, the alien-looking monster slurped away her insides. Then its repulsive voice echoed in my ears.

"*Sooo sweeet. The flesh is sooo sweeet.*"

* * *

Luis Rodriguez

My eyelids tore open. I ran to the bathroom and began to throw up. My heavy choked breathing, and retching, filled the quiet home. I splashed water on my face. *Lunar, get a hold of yourself.* It was just a hellish nightmare. I shambled back toward my moms' room. Something soaked my feet. . .

I hit the hallway light.

My feet gleamed with blood.

* * *

124
Luis Rodriguez

The bell rang. I quickly scuttled to the back doors. My bro-slices were waiting for me at the front of the school. Exhausted and anxious, I didn't want to speak with anyone but Chuy. To avoid my crew, I had to take the long way home. I ducked through some bushes and cut through an alley. I walked along a corridor of trash bins. Footsteps echoed around me. I turned back and saw no one. I must be hearing things now. Low snickering echoed. I clenched my fists, and looked behind me. Two scheming goons appeared.

"Well, well, well, I knew I smelled a chump. I hope you're ready for pay-back. No one makes a fool out of our crew without paying the price. Now it's time to taste a slice." Gee Slice flipped out a knife. "I brought Betty to this party, and Betty is hungry."

"Heheheehdidydeeheee."

Weasel's ear-bleeding laugh and Gee Slice's blade made my knees quiver. Bleep, how was I gonna survive this? "Fellas, I understand you're salty cuz Bola lost the duel. But that's the past. Bola and I are friends now . . . kind-ah sort-ah."

Weasel's smile melted into a scowl. "Lame-elio must think we're stupid to believe something so . . . stupid. It's time for him to bleed."

They stepped slowly toward me. I looked for an escape. They had each side covered — a trap. "Fellas, how about I give you a free dance lesson and—"

"Nuff talk, time to meet Betty," said Gee Slice.

They lunged toward me, and I assumed fighting stance. Vicious fists flew at me. A burning pain, like acid, covered my face. Blood poured down my cheek. I stepped back and threw out my arms to block the blows. Gee Slice whipped his knife across my other cheek. I felt acid again and then more blood.

"Oooo, Betty likes it."

I blindly kicked and punched with all my might. Then several boney knuckles pounded into my body. My flesh immediately swelled and I fell over. My ears rang. Everything went black.

Shhing. Shhing. Shhing. Shhing.

"Heheheehdidydeeheee."

"Hey, sleeping beauty is starting to wake up," said Gee Slice.

The awful voices of the two nalga breaths woke me. I couldn't move—wrapped in a duct tape cocoon like a helpless caterpillar. Apparently, I was in the middle of the abandoned lot where the high school kids smoked cigarettes. *Thud.* They rolled me into a hole. With shovels in their hands, the two goons began to laugh again. *Fffffp. Psshh.* Dirt peppered my face. The donkey-holes were burying me alive!

My brain went into panic-mode.

Steaming engine-oil-adrenaline pumped through my body. The metallic taste of blood coated my mouth. *Fffffp. Psshh.* More dirt poured on me and a small pile of it began to cover my body. My heart wanted to karate chop through my chest.

"Lame-elio, looks like you'll have the chance to find out all the gross stuff worms do to a dead body," said Weasel.

Gee Slice giggled. "Yeah! Maybe the chump will be able to *dance* his way out of this hole."

"Guys, you can't do this…I'll probably suffocate and die. *C'mon.*" I knew they didn't care, but I was desperate.

"Can't hear you, loser, too busy shoveling dirt," said Weasel.

Fffffp. Psshh. Psshh. The dirt fell faster still. My nightmares were coming true. I would be buried and forgotten. Soon I could expect teenagers peeing over my grave and littering it with cigarette butts. "Guys, please don't do this . . ."

"Heheheehdidydeeheee, I think he's gonna cry. We should be burying him in diapers."

"At least you'll be reunited with your *dad*," mocked Gee Slice.

Dirt fell over my mouth and eyes. Claustrophobia kicked in and I struggled to move.

Gee Slice gasped. "Hey, look who it is."

"Good timing, heheheehdidydeeheee. We're giving this loser a lesson never to mess with—Hey what are you doing? We're supposed to be boys—"

SMACK. SMASH. SWAP. BASH."

I heard the violent sound of bones cracking and tree branches breaking. I spit dirt and cigarette butts out of my mouth and tried shaking the muck from eyes. A large hand lifted me out of the hole.

"Lunelio–you ok?"

Oh. My. *Bleep.*

I never thought I would be so happy to hear that voice. Bola wiped the soil from my face and tore the tape from my body. So happy to be alive, I could barely feel my cuts and bruises. I looked for the two donkey-holes. Both were stuck in trees. Their limbs looked mangled and they whimpered meekly. Bola and I walked over to the dangling butt-clowns.

"Here's *your* chance for some payback."

Bola handed me a thick branch.

"Go ahead, whip their asses or somethin. These cowards deserve it."

I grabbed that branch like a chubby kid ready to destroy a piñata—took a few practice swings and heard the branch whisk through the air. Then I heard sniffling and soft crying. Weasel attempted to cover his tears, but it was futile. The fragile cries, like a baby, exploded into huge sobs. Gee Slice blurted out words that made us all gasp in horror.

"I . . . I . . . I—want my mommy."

No way did that just happen. Weasel covered his face gesturing a friendship denial while Gee Slice sprayed him with a waterfall of tears and snot. These two looked awfully pitiful. Bola's large face froze. I shook my head and dropped the branch.

"Looking at those two makes me sad. Let's get outta here or somethin."

I looked up at Bola. "*Word.*"

* * *

We reached the street that separated our neighborhoods. The words from Viorica's letter echoed in my brain. I took a deep breath. I had to say something to Bola.

"Hey — you saved my life."

"No big deal or nothin."

"That *is* a big deal." I reached out my hand. "I owe you."

We awkwardly shook, then I introduced Bola to my crew's secret handshake.

"Bola, this is thee sacred handshake. This handshake is an oath as strong as adamantium and it is also an invitation."

"Invitation?"

"An invitation to join my crew."

Bola shrugged and stuffed his hands in his pockets. Blood caked at my cheeks and a swollen body, I shrugged back.

"I'd better go — my abuelita is probably worried about me somethin. See you around."

"See you."

We took opposite directions. Never had I imagined inviting Bola to join our crew. French-kissing a shark, I would have seen as more possible. Today he saved my life. He didn't know this yet, but when we shook hands I silently promised I would pay him back. As our distance grew, hope and excitement sloshed in my stomach.

* * *

Chuy's house wasn't far. My wounds would trigger her to freak out, but better her than moms. A bag of frozen peas, a peanut butter chocolate shake, and I would be healed in no time.

The sunset and the sky grew dark. An ambulance siren blared in the distance. A cat in heat screeched behind shivering trees. I took out Chuy's spare key. She gave it to me after the incident. It made me feel grown-up.

I walked past the empty driveway. It was karaoke night and my tío and tía loved to hit the town and get behind a microphone and sing. They were actually pretty good, but Chuy always got embarrassed. I let myself in. I couldn't believe it, but I actually felt good. I guess smelling death's crappy breath and living to tell the story would do that to you. Anxiousness to share every detail with Chuy pulled at my sleeves.

I ran up the stairs, saw the door cracked open, and walked in. A chilly breeze scratched at my arms. The room stank of sewage and decay. My stomach revolted in knots. Emptiness filled the room and glass crunched under my shoes. *Blood* . . . lots of it. As if someone clumsily tossed a brimming jar in every direction. Books and glinting glass shards littered the floor.

I stared at the wall next to her bed. A giant claw had carved into it. In one of the indentations, I saw a piece of flesh threaded with hair. I collapsed to the floor . . . drew deep breaths for a few moments, and mustered some strength.

I searched her room for clues and found a note. Words were carved into what looked like a piece of leather coated in filth. The stench got worse and I pinched my nose closed. I read the note.

Hell — O there — BOOOY. Let's make a deal. You break the spell you placed on the suitcase and I will return your cousin with MOST of her SKIN left intact. Hmmm — as I carve you this tasty message, I can taste the fear from her blood on my tongue. Her blood is soooo sweeeet. And her pathetic heart trembles so rapidly, it might just . . . POP! You better hurry BOOOY. Souls hiding under defenseless flesh and bones are the tastiest. Especially the ones with her sweet blood. Hee-hee-hee. You better hurry BOOOY. I might just eat her anyway and devour your family one by one. I easily get bored waiting, BOOOOOY — DON'T let me get BORED. Meet me at the abandoned warehouse on the east side of town. I hope you enjoyed my letter. It's carved out of freshly wax-coated skin. DOES THE SKIN LOOK CHEW-Y?

P.S. HURRY BEFORE I CLAW OUT HER HEART RIGHT BEFORE HER EYES!

The skin-letter spontaneously caught fire. I ran to the bathroom and threw it in the sink. By the time I turned the faucet on, the letter melted into a gelatinous mess. My heart plunged to my ankles.

A Nerd Avalanche On Ancient Astro-Mythology & The Fate of Our Universe

I locked the door of my pops' study. The walls were thin and my little sis could easily eavesdrop on my room. My crew frothed with curiosity.

"C'mon Lunar, what the bleep is this all about?" Twitch circled in my room. "You givin us the heebie-jeebies dude."

"Twitch's point is valid," said Math. "We haven't had to have an emergency meeting since Twitch raced the high school kids on mountain bikes down the forbidden hill and flew into a tree."

"Duuude, that was epic. Especially when Hollywood yelled—"

"To infinity and *beyond*," said Hollywood.

"An ambulance transporting you to the ER and us thinking you died was *not* that epic," said Math.

Twitch nodded ironically. "Good times, my peeps."

"Really?" blurted Math. "was your pee bag exploding all over you also a good time?"

Twitch's face flushed a pizza-sauce red. "Math, stop interrupting Lunar. You're being rude, dude."

Math shook his head. "Lunar, debrief us please."

I took a breather and poured out every detail.

* * *

A long tense silence had filled the room. Hollywood grinded his teeth, Math broke his pencil scratching down some notes, and Twitch chewed his nails. "You sure it was *human* skin, dude?"

The thought robbed my breath. I pictured Chuy with her mouth taped shut, chained to a dungeon wall, and bleeding from an open wound the size of my palm. "Yes."

"This is not your average everyday darkness," said Hollywood. "This is... ADVANCED darkness."

Math stepped forward. "Agreed, Hollywood. We must meticulously mastermind a plan to rescue Chuy and send this evil thing back to whatever dark hole in hell it came from."

I felt hopeless. "How?"

"Yeah, Math. You gots a plan my man?" said Twitch.

"No."

I wanted to cry. The rest of my crew lowered their heads in defeat.

"Wait a second," said Math. "This all connects to your abuelita. Did she leave any information behind that could help us? Any books?"

"Only a book of spells. And it doesn't mention that crap-faced creature," I said.

"Damn it. Then we have no leads. We will have to go into this confrontation blind."

"We're pretty much giving this demon a kid buffet," said Twitch. "When he eats me, I hope he starts with my legs."

My hands shook. "This could be a death sentence. I can't let you guys do this."

"Every man dies," said Hollywood. "Not every man really lives."

Twitch glared at him. "You won't be singing that line when your body meat is being minced up by demon jaws."

"This is so bleeping unfair." I grabbed my dad's picture and tossed it against the wall — glass shattered

This stunned my crew. The mess made me feel even more helpless and angry. I grabbed another picture of him and smashed it on the floor. Then I completely lost it and threw anything in sight against the wall. I struggled to pick up one of my pops' awards. Bronze and heavy. I tossed it with all my might and the floor spat splinters. My crew hid behind me until I stopped. I wanted to keep breaking things, but fell over with exhaustion.

"Lunar, look," Math pointed. Next to me peeked a hole in the floor. Inside lay an old chest with my abuelita's name engraved on its battered lid.

* * *

Thwack. Math swung a heavy pipe-wrench and broke open the chest. Inside we found several books. They had leather covers, silver lettering with gold-edged pages and shrouds of dust. The titles read *Quantum Astro-Cosmology*, volumes I, II, & III. Math immediately opened one. The lettering boasted thick black font that jutted from the pages, as if the words were freshly tattooed to swollen skin.

Math touched the words. "Hmm...well, it's not braille, but I think I can decipher the words."

"Dude, this is sad," admitted Twitch. "We have perfect vision and I'm pretty sure you can read better than all of us, times fifty."

We waited, and forced silent-sandwiches down our throats. Every few moments Math interrupted the silence with *uh-hmms, oooohs, uuuus,* and *ahhhhs.* The sounds made me nervous and beads of sweat dripped over my butt crack. Finally, Math blurted, "This . . . is—*it.*"

"What the bleep did you find?" I said.

"Well, my fearsome bro-slices, we may have some answers. Take a look."

We huddled around the book. The pages were vivid and tangled with drawings of symbols and shapes. Several images looked to be from science books about outer space.

Math carefully touched each word, and read aloud. "In the beginning, there was the Cosmic Source; the root of all existence. It began to stretch and gave birth to two tribes. The Cosmic Shaman and the Cosmic Warlocks. One tribe had been designed to fill the empty space of the universe with galaxies, stars, solar systems, nebulae, and billions of cosmic curiosities. Meanwhile, the other tribe created the necessary elements such as hydrogen, helium, oxygen, nitrogen, carbon and the fundamental molecular chain reactions to birth and sustain life."

"What does all this gobblety-gook mean?"

"It sounds like an ancient myth about how the universe was created."

"Twitch, let Math continue," I said.

"The universe continued to expand at an accelerated velocity. Within the darkest corners of space, antimatter began to multiply at an unnatural rate. This accidental birth created the deepest of all evils. An evil born to do only one thing: devour all light. These entities are known as Stygian Omegas. They are mammoth black holes in the fabric of space with a ravenous hunger that is never-ending."

"Dudes, I'm not sure what the bleep all that means, but those things sound awesome."

"*Sssshh,* Twitch," we said as one.

Math's fingertips continued absorbing each word. "The tribe of cosmic warlocks had spent too much time in the darkness expanding the universe. They had lost connection with their roots; the Cosmic Source. One day they witnessed a Stygian Omega devour a solar system killing billions of innocent beings with one bite. The warlocks instantly became obsessed with such dark power."

We gazed at a picture of a giant black hole dotted with burning red eyes and large black teeth.

"Do these entities still sound awesome, Twitch?" said Math.

For the first time, Twitch had no comeback and Math read on.

"The Omega gave the Warlocks a taste of light and the tribe became infected with a fierce addiction. With little effort, the Stygian Omegas took control of the Cosmic Warlocks. The most forbidden of all the laws of the Cosmic Source; devouring light. This cannibalistic act is when the Warlocks de-evolved into Demons. This is how the war for the dire fate of the universe began."

"War for the fate of the universe?" said Twitch. "Dudes, I barely survive the war between me and wiping my butt."

I felt pale. "Guys, he's right. We're just a bunch of snot-nosed kids."

"Are you suggesting we stop reading through these books?" said Math.

I winced. I started to feel dizzy and sat down. "No. Maybe we'll find something that could help us save Chuy."

Math nodded. "Ok, crew, let's split up books, scan through them, and see what other important clues we find."

Each of us snagged a book and flipped through the pages. Any time we thought we found something valuable, we checked it out with Math. I found a page titled *How It Will End If They Win*.

Math gave it a finger-scan and then shared it with us. "Once the demons get access to the Grey Zone they will inevitably locate the Cosmic Source.

The Stygian Omegas will ambush and instantly devour it. The universe will then begin to collapse in reverse cosmic de-acceleration. Meanwhile the Stygian Omegas will have grown large enough to consume whole galaxies in fractions of a second. This will mark the beginning of the end — of everything."

"Math," I said, "I wish you never would have read that."

"Dude, that's IF they win — they probably will," warned Twitch.

The room stood quietly. My skin color and hair started to match. We resumed flipping through the books. I saw pictures of three-headed snakes, six-point stars, the universe, shapes in the form of people glowing blue and full of stardust, demons with swords riding on comets, and shaman with light lancing from their eyes. My mouth fell open and the book dropped to the ground.

"What is it Lunar?" said Math. "What did you find?"

I couldn't speak, so grabbed the book and pointed to the words.

The Only Way To Access the Grey Zone.

A picture of a key — the exact same one Pebbles swallowed before she died almost jumped off the page.

"Is that what I think it is?" I said.

"Holy shitake mushrooms…what is it?" said Twitch.

Math leaned closer. "Lunar, what do you see?"

"It's the key . . ." The pieces were finally clicking in my brain. Math grabbed the book. His hands carefully slid over each letter. "The tribe of shaman created the Grey Zone to protect the Cosmic Source. The Grey Zone is a quantum pathway of interconnected portals that exist underneath the universe's skin and serve as short-cuts to all the main points of the cosmos. If in danger, what would otherwise take billions of light years, the shaman could reach the Cosmic Source in fractions of a second. They understood the paramount importance and danger of the Grey Zone, so they created only one key."

"That was why that filthy demon stole Chuy," I said.

"We now know two important things," said Math. "Chuy is still alive because that demon wants the key. And, WE cannot allow the vile minion to get its claws on it."

"Wait, dudes," Twitch cut in. "You're telling me Lunar's little spell is what's stopping this thing from getting that key and destroying the universe?"

"That is accurate," allowed Math.

"Awesome." Twitch forced me to high-five him.

"I feel like we're on, like, the bleeding edge of history. Everything ahead of us is totally unknown and there's no guarantee that things are going to be all right. It's exciting, but it's also bleepin scary. Right?"

We looked at Hollywood.

"Right on, Mr. Adventure Time dude," said Twitch, high-fiving Hollywood.

"Math, any more clues?" I said.

"Yeah. The key to the Grey Zone is made of a rare material called iridium. Within its iridium body is Cosmic Source essence. This makes the key also a weapon. Unlocking the key would release an essence so powerful it could vaporize a Stygian Omega and a legion of its demons."

"Finally," I said, "some good news."

"Yea—ah, we're gonna win," sang Twitch.

Math cleared his throat. "The key can only be unlocked by Protectors of the Cosmic Source."

"Nope, we're still screwed dudes," I said. "I can't help but think we will be left bleeding as we meet the end of our short, sad lives."

"Hope is the only thing stronger than fear," said Hollywood.

"He's right," Math agreed. "We must keep searching."

"Holy smokes," blurted Twitch, "look what I found." He held a book.

I Immediately recognized the handwriting: my abuelita's.

"This last chunk of pages repeats the same thing over and over. Someone went a little loco."

"That's my abuelita's personal diary." I tore the book from Twitch's hands and several pages fell out. Stop the demon at all costs. Stop the demon at all costs. Stop the demon at all costs. Stop the demon at all costs. Stop the demon at all costs. Stop the demon at all costs. Stop the demon at all costs. Stop the demon at all costs. Stop the demon at all costs. Stop the demon at all costs. Stop the demon at all costs. Stop the . . . The phrase had been written easily over a hundred times.

I gathered up the pages and found two that had been torn from the cosmic books. The title's font, Our One Hope, seemed to bleed on the page. I read it to my crew.

"The Cosmic Shaman took post throughout the vast universe. In order to do this, they had no choice but to dismember their souls and scatter the pieces throughout the billions of galaxies. Within each galaxy, few planets were chosen. Pieces of the Cosmic Shaman were hidden within the infant belly of the chosen ones; also known as the Protectors of the Cosmic Source. All chosen ones wear the mark of the sacrifice. Their powers can only be unlocked by Thee Sacred Spell. Once the Protectors have the key, together, they can use its power to destroy the enemies of the Cosmic Source and save the universe."

"Sweet," said Twitch. "All we have to do is find these protectors, have them do all the work, and then we can get my future wife back."

"Bro, that's a dumb idea," I said. "How are we going to find them? It said they could be on any planet in the galaxy. That's like . . . a lot of planets."

"Ten to the 24th power of planets." Math scribbled the number down for us.

1,000,000,000,000,000,000,000,000. Our faces pinched with shock.

"So, our chances at finding them are impossible?" I said.

Math looked down. "Yes . . . unless—"

"Dudes, chill out," said Twitch, "I'm Googling it right now."

"Ok, I'm done with this stupid discussion. I'm not going to wait for never to find these Protectors while Chuy gets eaten alive."

Twitch shrugged. "Still looking."

In frustration, I accidentally balled up the page in my hand.

"Lunar, be careful, you're ruining our most important clue."

Math took the papers from my hand.

"What in tarnation?" Hollywood pointed at a picture.

Math sharply inhaled. "What is it?"

We gathered around and peered at a horrifying illustration of a demon eating children in a small village. In its claws were two kids with bloody stumps instead of arms and legs.

"Dudes, let me read this one," insisted Twitch. "Beware brave Protector-dudley dudes."

"Twitch!" We all yelled.

"Ok, ok. Party-poopers. Ahem . . . The demons show no mercy. They crave the taste of light. The Cosmic Source gave birth to all life forms. This means all living things are made of light. The demons yearn to devour the light within living things. The light that exists in the blood of the Protectors, demons thirst for the most."

He paused. "Glad we're not protector-dudes. We would be super-screwed."

"Enough of this cosmic junk," I said. "Are you going with me to save Chuy or not?"

Math nodded. "We leave tonight."

His words sucked the oxygen from the room. My palms sweated. "Good . . ." Thoughts screamed in my mind. Runaway! You have no chance of saving Chuy. You don't even know if she is still alive—save yourself.

"If hope can win," said Hollywood, "and it *can* bro-manos, then I'll choose to be here to fight for tomorrow to high-five you yesterday."

"Dudes, my future wife will be pissed," moaned Twitch, "if I don't go with you guys."

My bro-manos' brave eyes peered back at me filling the hollows of my bones with shame. I bit my lip and nodded.

* * *

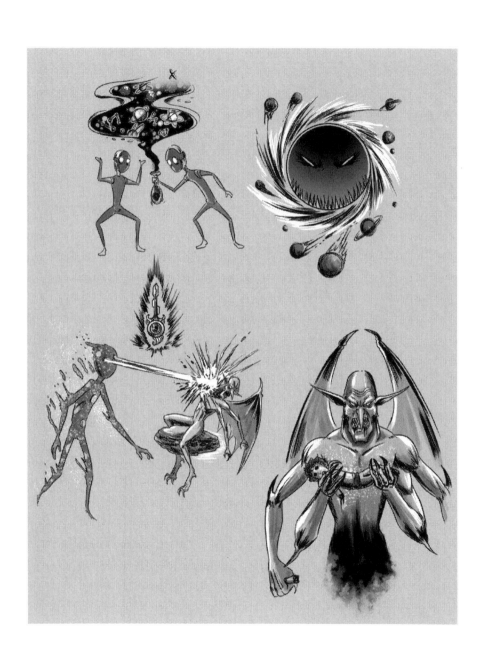

Luis Rodriguez

I left a letter for Viorica on my desk. Would I ever see her again? Would she ever read it? The word *hope* kept echoing in my mind. Sometimes Hollywood knew just what line to say. I felt terrible about my last moment with her. I let anger get the best of me and missed a chance to look at her one last time. I also left a letter for my moms and little sis. I had to let them know I had no choice and I loved them. My crew woke up and time began to rapidly melt away. I snuck into my little sister's room. I checked to see that she slept, gave her a gentle hug, and kissed her on the forehead. Two large eyes popped open.

"What is going on, Nelio?"

"Whoa, you scared me sis. Nothing is going on. Go back to bed."

"I heard you guys scheming in there. What are you up to? Why did you sneak into my room to give me a hug and a kiss? You haven't done that for years."

I paused and looked at her dewy brown eyes. She had gotten so big. It hurt that I might never see her again. I held her warm little hand. "Iolani, my bro-migos and I are going on a dangerous mission."

Her fingers clenched mine. "What is it?"

"All I can tell you is that Chuy is in big trouble. If we don't go save her . . . we will never see her again."

Iolani's eyes brimmed. "Why don't you tell mamà? She can call the police and . . ."

I caught one of her tears with my finger. "There is no time. I must leave *now*. Before I go, there's something you need to know . . . you're the best little sis in the world."

She threw her arms around my neck so tight I could barely breathe.

"If I don't come back, tell moms I love her."

Iolani punched my shoulder. "*Never* say that again. You *are* coming back and so is Chuy."

She wept. I planted another kiss on her forehead, and tip-toed from the room.

My crew and I looked at one another. I opened my bedroom window to night's black invasion.

* * *

We cut through several alleys. The gentle tapping of Math's walking-stick punctuated the darkness. My skin chilled. Confidence, razor-thin. I touched my pocket and felt my abuelita's book of spells—the only chance we had against the demon. IF, I could get the spells to work. As we scurried under the shadows, I silently rehearsed true magic incantations. I had no idea what the spells did—there were no explanatory texts, only the words Use Against Evil.

A dim light cut through the night's velvet blanket.

"Drop into an army crawl," whispered Math, "someone is near."

The rest of us dropped to our knees and carefully advanced. My chin scraped the ground, hands dug dirt. I bit my tongue to keep from complaining about old chewing gum getting stuck to my nose. The dim light brightened as we approached. A huge shadow loomed.

"You, we have been exsssspecting."

Out stepped a dog-sized rat with fur as black as death's teeth. It seemed to be hovering over us as it stood atop hundreds of its minions. The same rats Chuy and I encountered when Peebles had died.

"You four have made quite the grave decisssssion. You sssssseeeek to face a cosmic deeeeemon. Sooooo brave yet sssssso fffffoolish."

"Why don't you ugly turds go back into the sewer—"

"Hush, Twitch," rasped Math. "Under-dwelling friends, we have little choice. Have you come here to help us?"

"We have come here to fffffuuuuulfil our duuuuty. You have a friend watchhhhhing over you."

"A friend? What friend?"

"Enough quesssssstions. Iffff you prove worthyyyyy, you will get thee ssssspell."

"What spell?" I said

"Thee ssssssacred spell. Without it you are doooomed."

"Oooh, the sacred spell," said Twitch. "Dudes, what the bleep-balls is that ugly rat talking about?"

"I think it is the spell that would unlock the powers of a protector." Said Math.

"How does that help us?" I said. "Don't you need to be a Cosmic Protector to get those powers?"

Math scratched his head. "Lunar, I am as uncertain as —"

The king rat cut Math off. "It *IS* time to see if you are worthyyyy. Doooo you wear the mark of the sssssacrificcccce?"

A match sparked and a small flame illuminated the rat's face. It had no eyes. Instead, scars covered its eye holes. The fat rat moved toward us upon its legion.

"I will now gaaaaze into the passsst of you and your fffffriends."

The fat rat gripped my head with its crusty sharp claws. "*Aaaand* you *are coming witttth* meeeee."

I had an itch to punch that rat in the nose, but instead fell into trance as it spoke.

"Mmmm, leeeet me looook and ssssssmell into your mindsssss, Leeeeet me looooook and ssssssmell into your mindsssss. Leeeeet me loooook..."

My eyelids drooped . . . heavy and fogged. My heart gained a thousand pounds. The voice haunted my mind. The rat crawled among my memories . . . opened scabs of my past and bled them. I had lost my abuelita and then my dad. Chuy lingered next on the list . . . Tears boiled in my eyes and streaked my face as I watched images replay. I looked at my bro-manos trying to fight back tears as teeth bit into their lips and nails dug in their palms. I knew my bro-mano's darkest secrets just as they knew mine. We were all beginning to drown in the pain of our past. The ugly rat had invaded all of our minds and forced me to take a front seat on this tormenting ride.

My Bro-mano's Painful Past

One morning five years old Math awoke to his father cooking pancakes.

"Wake up your mamá," he said, "so we can have breakfast together."

Math gently brushed her shoulder. "Mamí, rise and shine." No movement. "Come on sleepy head." Carefully he grasped her shoulders and rocked her. "Mamí, wakey wakey." Still nothing. He instinctively lowered his ears closer to her face, and noticed the empty space where her breathing was supposed to be.

Math panicked and shook her with all his strength. His mom's head lifelessly moved toward him. He felt dry blood caked all over her ear and pillowcase—and screamed, *"Mamí, mamí, mamí!"*

His father crashed through the door. He pushed Math away, scooped up his wife, collapsed onto the bedroom rug and wept.

* * *

Twitch had only been a year old when his father left. The police had found Twitch just in time to save his little life. They carefully pulled him out of a wrecked vehicle littered with needles and stank of alcohol. Twitch's father had abandoned the scene of the crime and his only child. When Twitch's mom got the phone call she nearly had a heart attack. After months of hospital intensive care, baby Twitch and his moms returned to a completely empty house. His father took everything but the baby pictures. All Twitch ever learned of his father was that he lived as a petty thief and scam artist. His mom and half-dozen tías insisted they were better off. They would say, *he was ten percent man and 90% useless sin verguenza. That snake would sell his mother's bones for a quick buck.*

When we first met Twitch, his version of the story behind his father would constantly change.

"My old man was a fire-fighter-dude and died saving a baby. My old man was a construction-worker-dude and got crushed while building a skyscraper. My old man was an Airforce-pilot dude and died in battle." Then one-day Twitch said, "I don't know what happened to my dad. He was a drug addict, a thief, and a mega-cusshole. He's the reason I'm paralyzed from the waist down . . . I hope he falls into the sewer where all turds belong and gets eaten by an alligator."

This had been the one time we saw Twitch cry. We never asked questions, and Twitch refused to talk about him again.

* * *

At five years old, Hollywood watched his father treat his moms like a punching bag. His father's fists would slam into her face without mercy.

Hollywood would scream and shout begging his dad to stop.

He lost his first tooth biting his father's leg. His alcohol-reeking dad tore five-year-old Hollywood from his leg flesh and tossed the child into empty space. So many nights the home stank of blood and booze. Hollywood said this began his stuttering. He'd gouge teeth into his lips witnessing his mother's beatings . . . building trauma after trauma. No matter how loud he screamed, the bloody result always ended the same. Kindergarten is when the bullying started. Not knowing how to help him, his mom sat Hollywood in front of the TV and said, "Talk like *they* talk." He spent hours upon hours trying to learn to speak *normally*.

At school, they called Hollywood names like Stutters the monkey and Blubbering Berto. He would go home bawling, only to hear his mother weeping after being beaten. One day the neighbors called the cops. They found his mother half-dead — and took Dad away for good.

* * *

Luis Rodriguez

153
Lunelio's Epic Journey

My insides coiled in agony. The spell that rat cast on us made the moments a hundred times more intense. Reliving their past became unbearable. My crew and I couldn't take it any longer.

"Muh-muh-muh-muh-ma-ke hi-hi-hi-hi-hi-him st-st-st-st-st-op," cried Hollywood.

"Fat rat, that is enough! We have all bleeping sacrificed. Now give us the spell or watch the world burn," I said.

A long silence began to melt away the pain. It turned its bristly black head. "Child, I can sssssmell your suffffering miles away. But that doesssss not deem you worthy just yeeeet. You musssst next pass theeee test."

"What test?" I said

"Theeee tesssst, child."

Other rats rolled out a metallic box. Inside were three mice. They squealed helplessly. Like a switch-blade, the king rat flicked its long black tail. "Iffff its blooood is sweet the sssspell is yours. Iffff it is bitterrrr, fate will beeee unmerccccifuuuul."

"There must be another way," said Math.

"Yeah, furry dudes," Twitch shouted, "let the little dudes go."

"Stupid chhhhildren, shut uuuup. It is theeee only waaaay."

Without hesitation, the king rat sliced each mouse's throat. A chalice appeared and blood spilled over it. My crew and I cringed. All the rats hissed and squealed. "Silencccce."

The dirty rodent held up the chalice, and hushed its minions. With its filthy purple tongue, the rat licked blood from the cup's edge and curved form. Watching, the other rats hungrily licked their grimy snouts. Finally, the king chugged the blood. "Hmm. Hmmm. Hmmmmm…"

We waited painfully as the king rat swirled the blood in its mouth. Then I heard a revolting gulp.

"The blooood issss . . . sweeeet. They. Are Woooorrrrthy. Givvvve them the sssspell."

Rats climbed all over each other and approached us like a black hissing carpet. An oily paw handed me a scroll.

"Good luck proteeeectoooors of the Cossssssmic Ssssource. Stooooop the deeeemon and saaaave the unnnniverse. Fail, all woooorlds will commmme to an eeeend and you and everyyyyyone you love will diiiie."

The rats retreated into a jumbled black shadow, echoed an ear-stinging hiss, and disappeared.

"Thanks for the pep talk, fugly dude," said Twitch.

Hollywood nearly gagged. "Goodbye everyone, I'll remember you all in therapy."

"We have no time to waste, bro-manos," urged Math. "Lunar, read the spell."

I unrolled the scroll, scanned over the words, and began. My abuelita had taught me to trust that the true magic words would speak to me. Bizarre sounds unlike any other rolled off my tongue. I felt it to be someone else, not me, speaking. *"Det Nubis El Poder Et Paraciltus."* My pores began to rattle, and electricity surged through my body. Then . . . nothing. The wind and obnoxious crickets filled the empty darkness. No powers appeared.

"That stupid dirty rat lied to us the whole time. I'm gonna find him and kick him in the balls." Twitch got up from his wheelchair.

The rest of us gasped.

"What?" Said Twitch.

Then he saw.

"Holy donkey diarrhea."

"Bro, your legs — *work*," I said.

Twitch moved forward carefully trying to keep his balance. *"Dudes, I can walk! This is* awesome." He tested taking bigger steps, tripped on a rock, and...he vanished.

"Guys, what the bleep just happened to him?" I said.

I looked at Math. His smile shocked me.

"Something amazing, Lunar."

Zoom. Whooof. Twitch reappeared.

"Dudes, I can run really freakin fast. I'm pretty much the Flash only better-looking."

"Lunar," whispered Math, "your hair . . . it's glowing."

I pulled the tips of my hair close to my eyes. My old-man hairdo now shone a glimmering silver. My palms glowed blue. Abuelita's true magic words sang in my mind. Lifting my hands, I shouted, "*Deus Fuego!*" Blue fire speared the nightscape.

"Loon-balls, that's dab*tastic*," shouted Twitch. "Hey, where's Math?"

"Right here."

We looked around and saw nothing. Then out of the darkness Math materialized — as if he wore night as a camouflaging cloak.

"Bro-manos, these astonishing powers give us a fighting chance to end this battle in a victory dance."

Math's words lit me up. Rhyming meant Math regained his confidence. We turned then to Hollywood with excitement to see what powers the spell had given him. He shrugged as toads croaked beyond us, and opened his mouth to speak. But his tongue went haywire, as if ignorant of speech.

"*La. La la. La la la-figaro-figaro-fi-gaaar-ooo.*" Hollywood sounded like he prepared for the world's most epic opera performance. He continued singing and a shimmering pink ball appeared. With each sound, the ball got bigger until it completely enveloped him.

"Cool, I guess," said Twitch. "Hollywood can make huge girly-colored bubbles."

"That is no bubble." Math grabbed a large rock and threw it at Hollywood's face. *Brrsshh.* The rock exploded into bits. "That's a force field."

We all watched in awe. Math immediately dropped his walking stick, fell to the ground, and yelled in agony.

"Math, what's wrong?" I said.

Blood poured from the corners of his eyes. "I can *see* —"

"What? You got your vision back?"

"No, I can see into the *future* . . . the not-so-far future. We need to hurry. Chuy is dying."

* * *

BOLA'S CHAPTER

I had a stupid nightmare again. Always that gross orphanage. Sweat covered my shirt and my legs hung off my pathetic tiny bed. I could hear abuelita sleeping. Her snoring is loud and kinda scary. It sounded like to pigs wrestling or somethin. But I also kinda liked it because it meant she hadn't croaked on me. She's was old. Like super olden times old with pyramids and stuff. I realized I had to drain the weasel bad so went to the bathroom. I hate it when the toilet sometimes spits your own pee back at you. Like its angry or something. I splashed water on face. My face looked back at me in the mirror. Why was my face so big . . . so disgusting? Why was I born so ugly? Why was I even born?

I felt like punching the mirror into a thousand pieces. I would have too, except the noise could give my abuelita a heart attack or somethin. My stomach hurt like I ate a bunch of broken bricks or somethin. Then the lonely thoughts came back. They felt like mini-knives in my brain. I reached for the medicine cabinet to grab my pills. The doc called them my happy pills. I scooped a handful of the stupid weeny pills. I stared at them . . . stupid lame pills. The anger, like a dragon in my heart, took over. I crushed the weeny pills to dust and tossed them to the floor. The doc should have called them loser pills. No matter how many I swallowed, I still felt like a pathetic loser. The cabinet door hung open. Inside were my abuelita's beauty shop scissors. They were her favorite from when she cut hair like a hundred years ago. She used to cut my hair, but I hated it because she yanked more than cut. Every time I grabbed my pills the scissors looked at me, like a dare. They looked at me now.

I took them in my hand. They were ninja blade sharp at the point. I pushed one end to my wrist. Little pebbles of blood came out. This was easier than I thought it would be. I pushed the scissor deeper —

"Stop that."

I jumped and dropped the scissors. "I'm not doin nothin." I looked for my abuelita, but she wasn't there. Then I thought, hey that wasn't her voice. "Who said that?" Oh no, someone broke in again. I flexed my arms and made mean fists. I stomped to the front door ready to pounce anyone to death. A blue light appeared. A lady walked out from it like it was a door or somethin.

"Oh mijo, what were you doing?"

"Huh . . . nothin — none of your beeswax lady.

"Mijo, look at you, haven't you been through enough...."

"Lady don't call me that. Who are youdoin? What are you doin here?"

"Teyo, look into your heart. You will find who I am."

"Teyo? That's not my name. You must be drunk or somethin."

"Yes it is. Teyo, is the sacred birth name I gave you my beautiful child."

"Mamá . . . ?" The stupid word fell out of my mouth without my permission.

"Si, mi pollito." Before I could back away her hands touched my face. They felt soft and warm like marshmallows and sunshine. "I've missed you so—"

"No, you can't be . . . " I started to cry like a big baby. I couldn't help it. My body was doing stuff I didn't want it to.

"Mijo, I'm so sorry for how things turned out."

"You left me . . . in an *orphanage.*"

"Mijo, I never meant for that to happen. I did a terrible thing and betrayed my people. I tried to make things right and it cost me my life."

"You, *died?*"

"Yes."

So, you're like a ghost or somethin?"

"Yes."

"What about my dad?"

"The man that you could call a father was a treacherous coward. He also had to pay for his offenses with his life."

"So, I got no one . . . I am just a stupid freak— orphan.

"No."

The lady wrapped her arms around me. I would have pushed her a million miles away, but she was too fast. The hug felt like sunshine or somethin. Then I saw her face, those round eyes of an angel—

were the same from the picture in my locket. Could this really be her?

"My beautiful Teyo, you have a lovely woman that cares for you."

"I know, but she's old. Soon she will . . . will die — and I will have no one again." The stupid tears started again and I ran to my room. "Just leave me alone. I wish I was never born or nothin." A bright light came through my walls and there she was again.

"Teyo, never say those words again. I will always be a part of you."

"You will?"

"Yes."

She touched my hand. I felt weird . . . like almost kinda nice or somethin.

"My pollito, you have an important destiny."

"I do?"

"Yes."

"What . . . is it?

"Mijo, the universe is in danger. You have been chosen to protect it."

"I have? That's sounds nutty, who would choose me to protect anything?"

"Mi Teyo, there is little time. The source of all existence has a dark enemy that wants to destroy it. Doing so would end in the annihilation of all universes. For the first time in billions of light years, the darkness has a chance to achieve this horrible plan. You must help your friends to stop this. You can help save all worlds. You can turn your life around and become the hero you were *meant* to be."

"Me, a hero? Sounds like a bad joke or somethin."

"It sounds like your destiny Teyo."

I scratched my head. It felt like a heater had been turned on. So much happening too fast. What was this lady talkin about? Her big angel eyes glowed in my face. I wanted to hug her and tear my face off at the same time. Then I heard that laughter again—the orphanage punks. "How come you waited so long to find me?"

"Mijo, I exist in spirit form. Only the most powerful magic could create a doorway to find you. Your friends read the sacred spell and now its power flows through you. I've held on to one last grain of magic in hope that one day I would unlock such a door . . . a door to *you*."

Tears that looked like bitty diamonds fell down her face. I wanted to believe her so bad . . .but—the laughter got louder

"No, I won't believe your crazy lies. I don't have any friends and I don't need a new family or nothin."

"Mijo, please—"

"Stop calling me that lady. You left me to rot in an orphanage that was like a prison or somethin. This stupid universe will have to *choose* another loser to protect it. It's never done nothin good for me. Now go away."

"Mijo, only when you let go of your anger will you be free. This is your only chance to fulfill your destiny."

I looked the other way.

"Please know that I love you, and always will."

I felt more sunshine and then the room felt empty.

"Wait . . . come back. Don't leave." Freakin damn it! *BERRSH.* I punched the stupid wall.

"Mijito, what's going?" My abue's voice came from her room.

"Nothing abue. Just another nightmare. You can go back to bed."

Whoa, my fist went right through brick. I looked at my knuckles and didn't see a scratch. No way — *Thump. Thump. Thump.*

Oh no, I heard abue wobbling to my room. I quickly covered the hole in the wall with my pillows. *Tap. Tap. Tap.*

"Mijito, can I come in?"

"Uh . . . Okay abue." I didn't like ever saying no to her or nothing. She came in, sat next to me on my bed, and gave me the squinty eyes with her wrinkly face.

* * *

Is This Thee End?

We crept up to the abandoned building. A dilapidated tower of crumbling brick, broken windows, rusting pipes, and countless pitch-black corners glowered at us. My crew and I were tensely crawling around the perimeter ready at any moment for something to pop out and attack us.

"*Bro-manos*," Math whispered. "*Twitch and I will slip through the back of the building. Lunar, you and Hollywood will sneak through the side entrance.*"

I watched Math camouflage himself into the night and disappear. Twitch zoomed off. Treacherous darkness surrounded Hollywood and I. Fear's cold hands began to make my heart clatter. I pointed forward and we gently moved on. Each of our footsteps held its breath. We reached the rusty doors. I whispered, "*Spiritum Autem Dios Aperta*," and exhaled blue magic on the rusty hinges. The doors silently opened, and Hollywood and I scuttled in. Darkness, festering meat, and mold greeted us. I felt like I might drown in the stench.

KCKAAUUURRRLLLKK . . . CRACK . . . CRUNCH, CRUNCH, CRUNCH.

The sound of bones being minced by giant teeth sent shivers through every pore in my body. Were we too late? I snatched my flashlight and we frantically raced ahead. The light revealed piles of cracked ribcages, broken pipes, skull fragments, corroded equipment, and chunks of spine. We reached a labyrinth of pipe pathways connected by stairs.

"Aaaaaaahhhhhhhhh . . ."

The scream — *Chuy.*

"Get your hands off my future wife you turd Dumpster."

We heard the echo of Twitch's voice. Chuy's cries became louder. Hollywood and I spotted he and Math near a large circle of candles.

Math pointed to a cloud of black smoke. "The insidious demon was there a moment ago. It has the power to *teleport.*"

The tall sticks of wax burned bright. In the corner under a blazing fire there stood a black cauldron. The stink of dead flesh grew stronger.

"Glad you could make it boooy. I can *smell* your blood. The light in it smells soooo sweeeet."

I couldn't see where its voice came from. Then it appeared within the circle of candles.

"There is something I want to show you, tasty bags of flesh."

Like pulling a rabbit out of a hat, the monster gingerly displayed slabs of flesh. Torn holes and scratches covered the ragged skin-suit. It looked as if the meat of something, or someone, had been sucked out.

"Mr. Frutos, you are being rude. Say hello to the boooys."

The Dark Warlock mimicked a high voice. *"Hello, boys."* The slabs of flesh flopped about slapping the cold dirty ground.

"You remember Mr. Frutos, don't you BOOOY?"

Its eyes viciously fixed on me.

"The pathetic fool thought he could stop me; stop the inevitable. I enjoyed eating him alive. The screams added to the savory taste. But his cries for mercy were a nuisance. SO, I TORE OUT HIS TONGUE AND ATE IT AS HE BEGGED ME TO END HIS LIFE."

The demon tore the flab of skin in half and threw it on the ground.

"The skin is not satiating without the meat. I keep it for the *aroma*."

Sweat slid down my forehead and my hand grew clammy. Images of a brutal death for all of us flashed in my mind. Math elbowed my arm.

"Lunar, you must stay focused. The abhorrent creature attempts to weaken us with fear."

"How insightful, insignificant blind boy."

The dreadful thing turned to Math.

"You have no eyes to see, yet can see better than most. What a delightfully and pitiful irony. You think your powers will save your lives? THEY WON'T."

"I know why I'm here," I said. "I know why you stole the suitcase and took Chuy."

"Do you? *Tell* me."

"You want the key. You want to use it to destroy the universe."

"Heeheehee, *and*?"

"And—we can't let that happen. The key belongs to *us*."

"Boooy, I helped create this pointless universe. It has long reached its expiration date."

"Vile demon, be prepared to taste our wrath," declared Math. "You will regret ever crossing our path."

"That's right, you ugly-mugly-fugly. Lunar isn't giving you shi—"

"*Aaaaaaheheheheheheeheehee!*"

The demon's high-pitched laugh shook the entire factory.

"The weak, the blind, the cripple, and the mute have come to stop me. Priceless and utterly futile."

The demon vanished.

Chuy's desperate cries silenced, and a violin keened. I looked up and saw an immense mechanism with gears and winding wheels. It resembled the inside of a watch, but thousands of times bigger. At the top of it, I saw Chuy, wrapped in chains. Her clothes were caked in blood and gashes covered her whole body. Some of her wounds were fresh. I watched her play the violin. Chuy looked like a marionette puppet, face bone-white, movements jerky and unnatural. The nightmare sound of the music she played made my pores shiver.

"The dreadful creature is trying to distract us," noted Math. "Chuy is under a dark spell."

"You *stupid* morsels of flesh. Give me the key, and maybe die with mercy."

Its voice came from every corner, but all we saw were shadows. Fury surged through me and blue fire crackled in my palms. "Show yourself, coward!"

"Peek-a-boo."

The demon materialized behind us—and vanished. The back of my neck abruptly burned, as if injected with venom. I touched it and found a gash, blood oozing from it. The rest of my crew bled too.

"The light tastes so sweet— ooheeheeheeheeheehee. So sweet—more I must have."

The demon reappeared. It hovered in the air before us, long razor-sharp claws dripping our blood. Math disappeared. Twitch zoomed off. Blue fire fumed in my hands and Hollywood began to sing.

"*Fuego Autem Draco!*" The words of true magic exploded from my mouth and flew like a giant fireball toward the demon. Twitch, faster than the speed of sound, flung hundreds of rocks at it. *BRRRRSSHH.* My magic and the rocks smashed into the wall. Damnit, we missed. The demon teleported above our heads and flew at us with its deadly claws aimed for our throats.

"*I see trees of green, red roses too. I see them bloom for me and you. And I think to myself . . .*"

Hollywood's forcefield quickly wrapped around us as he sang. *BOOOM*. The demon crashed into us. The impact sent it through a cement wall. The forcefield began to crack and I noticed Hollywood's nose and ears dripping blood.

"*…what a won-der-ful world…*"

"Hollywood, this song?" I said.

"It's my mom's favorite."

Math rematerialized. "His choice is of no matter. He must make sure this force field does not shatter."

Hollywood nodded, and Math dissolved back into the darkness.

"You annoying runt. I'll use those legs as tooth pics."

Twitch, only a blur, swirled around the demon's legs and whipped the evil thing with a metal chain. Black sludge began to leak from its wounds. The demon lashed its claws at Twitch, but couldn't catch him. The demon shrieked and then teleported. *Zwoosh.* Twitch returned to my side.

"Safe at home base."

"*I see skies of blue and clouds of white*
The bright blessed day, the dark sacred night . . ."

The force field began to get larger and the cracks started to fade.

Twitch grinned. "Kickin demon ass is awesome."

A petrifying shriek made the ground tremble. *BOOM.* The demon collided into the force-field again. This time the whole field filled with cracks. One more crash and ours would be demolished. I looked at Hollywood. He smiled as blood dripped from his eyes and forehead.

"And I think to myself, what a wonderful world . . ."

"Twitch, we need to do something," I said. "This is killing him."

The demon reappeared above us, and Twitch zoomed off. I clenched my teeth and called the true magic to my hands. Electricity popped from my palms. The demon kamikazed at me. Twitch wrapped the chain around its throat, Math appeared and shoved his cane through the creature's right eyeball, and my hands exploded. "Fuego Autem Draco!" *BRRRRSSH.* Blue light ate darkness. The demon flew through another wall and flopped to the ground. Rains of debris echoed and boomed through the building. Then silence. Twitch zoomed off again. "Twitch, get away from it," I said.

"I think it's dead." He poked it with a length of jagged pipe, and black sludge welled up from the wound. "Gross, its eyeball is all smooshed and nasty, dudes." The demon lay limp.

Twitch stood over the thing. "See, it's not moving."

Math closed his eyes. "Stand back, Twitch, I am receiving a future image." Abruptly his face tightened with dread. "Twitch — *run!*"

"*Aaaaaahehehehehheeheehee.* Stupid *booooy.*"

The demon clamped its claws onto Twitch's leg. "*Aaah*, get *off* me."

Twitch's free leg, like rapid-fire, kicked the demon's face. I ran toward them, electric blue crackling in my hands.

Twitch screamed. "*Aaaaaaahhhh.*"

The demon had snapped his leg like a pretzel stick.

His dead ankle swelled, dangled useless weight. The creature ripped the cane from its eye socket. Black gunk sprayed Twitch. The demon howled.

"*Vil Tenebris Victa!*" I blasted the thing again — it dropped Twitch and vanished. Math appeared — dragged Twitch our way. Hollywood resumed his song, and the force-field pulsed around us like a massive pink shell.

"*The colors of the rainbow so pretty in the sky,*
are also on the faces of people going by.
I see friends shaking hands saying how do you do,
they're really saying —"

The demon materialized before us — claw working a shrinking hole in our force-field.

Kkksss. It sliced Hollywood's throat; blood gushed. The force-field could be seen dissolving. Math tore a strip from his shirt, tourniqueted Hollywood's wound. The bleeding wouldn't stop. Hollywood's convulsed, and Twitch howled in agony nearly as fierce as the demon's laughter.

"You son of a bleep." Blue fire speared from my hands.

The monster teleported and my magic punched through the wall. Cement chunks smashed to the ground. I lifted Twitch to his good foot, and we hobbled toward Hollywood and Math.

"Oh no, dudes," Twitch cried. "Hollywood is looking grossly pale. We can't let him *die*."

Math shook his head as if in denial. "The bleeding is subsiding. Wait, I'm getting another vision."

I could see those intelligent eyes widening behind the shades.

"Dude, what is it?" demanded Twitch. "You're giving us a constipation face."

"I . . . I just watched us die."

I shook my head, dizziness fizzing in my skull. "Math, that can't be . . . " "*Aaaaaahehehehehehhehheeheehee.* You pathetic babies. *Yes,* you are all going to die and it's going to taste *sooooo sweeeeet.*"

The demon raged, flew at us.

Gravity's law suspended itself—I spun into empty air like a Styrofoam cup. The four of us whirled, lost in a seeming tornado of razored claws slicing and stabbing—blood sprayed the earth, and the demonic shrieks hammered my ears.

"You, stupid boooyy, get ready to *die* like your grandmother. *Aaaheeheehee!*"

My veins surged with hate and rage—and a last true magic hit failed. Weakness owned me. I could hear my bro-manos crying out for mercy.

"*Please*," wailed Twitch, "make this thing *stop*, Lunar."

This was it, our end.

We failed. *I* failed.

There — I could see Chuy. Tears shone bright in her eyes. The monster licked our blood from its jagged fangs.

"What a satisfying appetizer. Boooy, now it's time for you to open that suitcase. How you follow my instruction will decide the *type* of death all of your loved ones will endure."

The wretched demon teleported to Chuy. Fear-acid ate at my stomach walls. Under the demon's spell, Chuy stroked the violin's strings, face rigid with terror.

Terror I shared — the demon whipped a taloned hand, gripped Chuy's, and bit through a finger.

Chuy screamed — so did I.

Blood spattered her face, the violin, jetting in sympathy with her racing heart. How could she survive?

"*You cowardly bleep!*" cried all of us.

With a finger-snap, the demon had Chuy resume her dark music. It grinned at us.

"I WILL *EAT* THIS HELPLESS CHILD BIT BY BIT UNLESS YOU DO AS I SAY."

"Okay," I said, "you win . . . Tell me what to do . . ."

"Go to the corner on your right. Underneath those pipes, you will find the suitcase. Go . . . and open it."

I found the suitcase, a battered thing smeared with filth and mold, dragged it toward the dark son-of-a-bleep. I had to fight against puking from the overwhelm of rotten flesh. I cupped my mouth with a bloody hand, ransacked my brain for the spell, body a symphony of pain vibrating with Chuy's keening violin. Fear sandwiched my mind.

"HUUUURRRRY BOOOOY."

The demon's eyes burned red as it drew rivulets of blood from Chuy's neck. Needles and static flowed through me — my form hummed. The words popped and snapped from my tongue. "*Llave Autem Dei, Aperta.*"

Click. I opened the suitcase and gasped.

Buzzing flies boiled out from the dog carcass on which they — and legions of maggots — had been feeding.

Thwack. The cosmic monster thrashed my face — sent me flying.

I slammed into the ground.

The thing's black claw punched through stewing insects and bone, levitated with a triumphant spread of its arm. Towering above, it rained down laughter and foul debris.

"Finally, the beginning of *THE END.*"

The key shimmered in the creature's grasp.

Luis Rodriguez

Distracted by this sight, I missed the demon's snake-quick thrust — and got clamped in its claws and raised high. "Let us go…*please*."

"Aaahh — how PATHETIC. Begging for mercy! Boy, deep inside, you had to know you came here to die. Your life belonged to me years ago. You've been living a dream, stupid booooy."

"Why are you doing this? You guys used to be *good*. If you do this, everything will be destroyed, including you and your kind."

"*Ahhahahaheeheehee. You* are lecturing, *me*? You're speaking of things which you know not, boooy. And I find it *boooring*. Your friends now get to watch you die."

A claw stabbed my chest.

178
Luis Rodriguez

"*Nooooo!*" My crew screamed through Chuy's death-track to my end. I envisioned our families burying us in empty caskets . . . my little sis's despairing tears raining into a dead man's box with no . . . *me*. I'm sorry crew. I'm sorry Chuy. I'm sorry moms. I'm sorry little sis. I'm sorry abuelita. I'm sorry Viorica. I'm sorry pops . . .

* * *

Bola Chapter 2

Abue would not leave my room. I wanted to be left alone. Her wrinkly face looked at me for like forever or somethin.

"Mijito, there is something we need to talk about."

"Abue, can we do this talk tomorrow —"

"No mijito, we are having it *now*. Look at me."

Her saggy face came close to mine.

"I'm not sure how many tomorrows I have *left*."

"Don't say that, you're not that old or nothin."

She smiled one of her sad smiles and put her hand over mine. Her fingers were boney and felt scratchy.

"Do you remember when I picked you up from the orphanage?"

"No . . . maybe . . . I guess."

"Your eyes looked so angry and lost. They tried to convince me not to take you home. They said I was too old and you were too angry. But I didn't listen to them. Do you know why?

"Why?"

"Because I knew behind those angry eyes was so much pain. I felt with my love I could heal you, and the pain would go away."

"Please don't cry abue —"

"After all these years, there's still so much anger in you mijito. Your eyes are still filled with pain. I was wrong thinking my love could *change* that."

"Abue, I love you. I . . . I'll be *better.*"

"Mijito, then let it go. It's time to stop carrying that pain."

I didn't know what to say or nothin. So, I just stared at my jumbo feet.

"Your mamá came to visit me once. I knew it was your mamá the moment I saw her. She had your eyes. She appeared a month after I brought you home. She thanked me and told me your birth name. I'm sorry I kept it a secret all these years. She walked right through these walls. I couldn't tell if it was a dream, her ghost, or me going loca. But just now, I heard her speaking to you . . ."

Abue's words made my heart feel like it had just been punched. My legs then started to turn to jelly. I fell with my back against the wall and slid to the floor.

"Teyito. I always knew you were special. Whatever she told you . . . your mamá — please *listen.*"

I closed my eyes. I could still hear them laughing. I could still smell that stinking place.

I opened my eyes. Oh no! The orphanage gray hallway waited for me like it wanted to eat me. Footsteps took me by surprise. I jerked my head and readied my fists. Mrs. Love walked up to me with an angry face and flicked her bird nose. She liked reminding me she was the boss.

"Mop all the rooms *now*."

Mrs. Love hit me with a ruler if I didn't mop fast enough. I could hear the other kids meeting parents in the front room. Sometimes the anger in me got so strong I felt fire in my skin. I felt like an explosion of hurt or somethin. I threw the broom at the window and screamed like a dragon. I was trying to rip the anger from my insides or somethin. Glass covered the ground, my throat burned, and almost-parents ran. Mrs. Love slapped my face, pulled my ear to the basement, and left me there for days. When I wasn't in the orphan dungeon, I hid in my corner and watched new parents smile at their new kids.

"You are going to love your new home."

From the front window, I watched kids get in their new car and drive away to their new life. I tried to keep the tears in my eyes but couldn't. I felt like dying or somethin. Mrs. Love stood over me breathin mean like an animal or somethin.

"You keep acting like a beast, and you'll be an orphan forever."

I rocked back and forth and put my hands over my eyes to hide from her. She finally stomped away.

I had one safe place, the garden. Mrs. Love stayed away because of all the misquotes buzzing around. I caught tiny frogs by the pond and then set them free. They were my only friends. Then one day lame punks ambushed me or somethin. Two big ugly ones sat on top of me. Their fat asses squished me, I

couldn't breathe. Another punk kid found one of my frogs. He made a fist and crushed it dead. One of its little eyeballs popped out and blood came out of its mouth. I wrestled like a snake or somethin to get free. Then the fat ugly smooshed the dead frog in my face. Anger filled up in me like a balloon and I was ready

to pop. I wanted to hurt those kids into the hospital or worse . . .

I could see Mrs. Love's face again. She always looked down at me and yanked my chin. Her breath smelled of coffee and old eggs or somethin.

"*Look* at you. All you do is scare moms and dads away."

I hid my eyes in my hands. I had wished to explode so all my gross guts could splatter all over her.

My memory then took me to that night in my bunk bed. I bit my lip and made fire fists. Kids surrounded and threw me to the floor. They jumped on top of me and covered me with duct tape. I tried to scream. I tried to get free. They laughed and laughed.

"You have to *pay the price* for being the ugliest kid here. All you do is scare parents away. It's *your fault* parents haven't come to take us home. *You* must pay. Now drink the warm lemonade."

More kids joined in. "*Drink. Drink. Drink. Drink.*"

Luis Rodriguez

I held my breath. They took turns peeing on me. Anger filled up in me like lava in a volcano or somethin. I wanted to bash each of their heads.

The voices were so loud now.

You're disgusting. Your parents abandoned you. You're too ugly to be loved. You're so pathetic. Why were you born? You were an accident. Go ahead pick up those scissors. They're sharp enough you ugly muck. No one will care. No one will miss you. No one —

"Stop!" The whole house shook and the voices shut up.

"I am not ugly . . . I am not pathetic . . . I . . . am Teyo. My mamá loved me. My abue loves me. I have a destiny!"

Abuelita smiled up at me with tears falling over her cheeks. I stood up. My body began to glow or somethin. I closed my eyes again. This time I didn't see a memory. I saw something else . . . Lunelio and his friends.

"Oh no —"

* * *

GOODBYE

"*Aaaaaah* — what is *that*?"

The monster tore open my shirt, and I looked down. No blood!

In a burst of hope, I saw its claw had cracked open Viorica's charm. Purple light lanced out — spread holy fire over the demon's flesh like a vampire under the sun.

"It *BURNS!*"

The monster bolted into the air — taking me too.

"You are full of *tricks*, aren't you BOOOOY. It is of no consequence, she is too late to help."

The evil creature tore out its melted claw, flung it away. Black sludge sprayed my face — trinket hit the ground in pluming purple smoke.

"Goodbye, pathetic boooy."

Its remaining claws clutched my neck like razored snakes. *THWACK.*

Fog. My mind drifted . . . body flailed falling for the cold earth. Tumbling to my death, the demon's words confused me. Then I saw broken fangs flying! *BOOF.*

"Are you okay, Lunelio?"

I looked up. "Bola...?"

Bola cradled me in his behemoth hand. I stared blankly. He looked as if he had been showered and polished. A glow beamed from his body as if a giant night light burned inside of him.

"Lunar we don't have much time. We have to stop this gross thing or somethin."

I nodded and began to focus. Twitch held on to Hollywood, a pale bag of skin.

"The disgusting orphan no one wanted has arrived. Do you know who I AM? I'll give you a clue, orphan. I can still taste your *mother's* pitiful blood."

The demon sniffed its claws in mockery, even indulgently licked them. "Sooo soo *sweeet*, and *painful*, was her death."

Gnarled arms, writhing like snakes, sprouted from its ashen skin. Claws snapped like teeth. This abortion of reality morphed into what might have been a spider from some galactic cellar. My fingers and arm, as if needled by fire ants, buzzed with electric blue fire. My palms glowed, and I turned to Bola, whose body swelled and swelled like a weather balloon—easily tripled in size.

"You inferior bags of flesh are too late, I have the key!" The demon raised its claws, chanted ancient words. A cloud of fiery red and black embers gushed from its maw. A swirling vortex—or portal?— glowed over our heads.

We stepped back.

Bola's bloated body became a luminous orb, pulsing blue fire. He glared, and my hands flamed. Bola lunged at the demon.

I hollered, "*Ignis De Dios!*"

BOOOOOSSSHZZ. An explosion flashed— jagged debris shredded air. The creature flung itself .

.. and bashed into a wall, scattering stones and crumbled mortar.

"Dudes," Twitch managed, "we have to *close* that portal."

"We need the *key*," I said.

Math popped from the dark, hand silvery. "We are back in destiny's seat. Defeat, we must make this sinister creature meet. Not even in the face of death will we retreat."

Hope surged, and I said, "Bola, get Chuy—"

Before I could finish, Bola leaped high—landed atop the massive gears to which she was chained. *RRRRTURFFF.* Chains snapped—echoed through the vacant factory. Cement dust peppered the ground.

A pair of enormous feet smacked the floor in front of us. Bola carefully cradled Chuy in his muscular arms . . . gently settled her form on the ground. Her labored breath tried to form words through the heavy mask of blood and grime. "Oh my gosh—Oh my gosh . . . Lunelcito . . ." She gasped for air. "I thought . . . the nightmare would never . . . *end.*"

I gave her a bear hug. "You're with us now."
BOOM.

The Dark Warlock erupted from the cement floor. Debris shot everywhere.

"The bags of meat finally reunited? How *pointless.* Blind bow, you have something that belongs to me. Give it back. *Now.*"

Bola jumped in front of us. The insidious thing vomited the most awful cackle.

"Aaahhhhheeheehee! Is the pathetic orphan going to save the universe or *die* like his stupid mothe—"

Bola's giant fist cracked into the demon's face and sent it through the air. Fangs and black sludge flew. The monster howled—teleported.

"You insignificant peons will die— excruciatingly. Now, give me that *key*, blind boy!"

The demon reappeared and reached for Math, who instantly camouflaged into the darkness. Bola smashed the creature's face with a fist. The demonic monster again teleported and Bola missed.

"*Ignis De Dios*!" I blasted the demonic turd again—no direct hit. Like a hellish dream stuck on repeat, this dance continued.

"Lunelio, we need to hurry," urged Chuy. "Roberto is dying."

I turned to them. Hollywood's pupils dilated.

"*Dudes*," cried Twitch, "we need to get him to a hospital—pronto. I can barely hear him breathing."

I didn't know what to do.

BOOOSSSH. The monster collided with Bola.

The impact knocked us off our feet. The creature attacked Bola like a hurricane. Razored claws sliced him. Bola bombarded the demon with punches like comet impacts. Blood and black gunk spattered walls with abstract paintings of our torment. Bola struggled with whirling dust, debris, and blood.

"*Noooooo* – Ignis De . . ."

Like fumes from a dying engine, I saw effervescence of my spell fade. My true magic had been drained, again. Fear burned in my heart. I turned to Chuy. Her eyes glowed. Oh bleep, the demon put her under another spell. She beckoned with her arms . . . opened her hands, and roared. "*Nebulosa Bumerang Basium!*"

Blue light beamed from her mouth and eyes – iced the demon's charcoal legs.

No way, Chuy just cast a –

"Aaaaahhhhh! Annoying bag of flesh, I should have *killed* you!"

The demon's starry red eyes daggered Chuy. As its python arms slashed at Bola's face, he caught them and yanked. Veins popped out of Bola's muscles as he pulled with all his might. *RRRRRRRRPPP.* The demon's arms flew off. Then Bola grabbed another pair and tore them from their sockets. Sludge spewed like an open fire hydrant. The demon fell over, finally showing a sign of defeat.

"Aaaaahhhhhheeheeheeheehee! You stupid bags of flesh cannot stop the inevitable. We will win and this universe will fall. Everyone you love will *die*."

Thunder cracked behind us. We turned to the portal. Demons crossed its threshold, one of which was ringed with eyes. Another had none. One a had a huge fleshy slot from which it shrieked. A tentacled worm crowned with rows of jagged teeth churned the soil, another spread massive bat-wings. A blob-shaped terror had an open torso studded with needle-teeth. Twitch's wide eyes broadcast horror. "Dudes, we are so freaking *screwed*—"

Pprrrrssh. A cloud of purple erupted.

Air swished—sundered by a sword bright with electric charge. Abruptly the blob-demon whined—and split apart in an explosion of meaty chunks.

Bloody mist fogged the space, and through it I picked out a silver shield, blurred armor, and—what?—a swirl of purple hair. It couldn't be real. It couldn't be true . . .

I peered deeper. "It can't be—"

Twitch's eyes crossed. "Dude, that is *totally* your girlfriend. Holy ssshh—"

"*Lunelio,*" ordered Viorica, "you need to open the key's cosmic light."

She hovered high like a magical knight. Enchanted, I stood paralyzed.

"Lunelio, *now.*"

I snapped out of my brain-freeze. "Twitch and Chuy, keep Hollywood safe. We are *ending* this."

Hollywood managed to give me a thumbs-up. I scanned the ruined landscape for Math.

He stumbled from a smoldering flesh-pile. "Lunar, a guardian angel has just resuscitated our fate, there is no time to *wait.*"

He handed me the key. "You can and *will* do this."

192
Luis Rodriguez

I nodded and swallowed hard. Before my eyes, Bola ripped the limbs from other demons as Viorica sliced them to bits. More slithered from the portal. I took the key, flesh crawling with fright. I had to get this right and I had no idea *how*. Four demons surrounded Viorica and attacked.

"Lunelio, *hurry!*" she screamed.

"Iubes Me La Luz Autem Fons Mundi," I cried.

Time froze.

I felt abuelita's profound presence . . . witnessed the birthing of the universe. Atmosphere, for the first time, pulsed and exhaled. I saw the first-born green leaf . . . first rippling stream . . . wriggling one-celled organisms fighting for breath . . . the first silvery star falling through space . . .

The key expanded into a wave of white light— and took Viorica with it. Demons fractured into infinite shards . . . sucked into whatever lower dimension birthed them.

My legs gave out and I collapsed . . .

At once Viorica stood over me, sword, shield and armor mirror bright. Black gunk dissolved from her battle gear. "You *did* it."

With her warm hand, she lifted me to my feet.

"No, *we* did," I said.

I gazed into her steady, unwavering eyes. Unearthly irises gleamed with crystal purity, like purple diamonds. Our lips brushed. My insides melted like clouds—fireworks boomed, blossomed into star-wheels. It was my first kiss . . .

"Who are you?" I said.

"Lunelio, I am from another world. It was once a small and beautiful planet. Now it has been taken over by Cosmic Demons. The monsters killed my father and mother. With the king and queen vanquished, it took little time before my land fell under their control."

"Wait, king and queen? That makes you . . . a princess."

"In order to be a princess, I must have land to serve and protect."

"Your Highness," gushed Math, "are you saying you came to our planet to retrieve the Cosmic key?"

"It's the most powerful weapon to use against them. With it, I could free my land and my people."

I couldn't stop looking at her. "I still don't understand. Why did you leave?"

"My little sister was being hidden by my people. The demons found Lucia. I had to try and save her."

"Is she safe now?" said Chuy.

"No, but she is still alive. I can feel her energy. On my rescue mission, I..."

Viorica fixed me with that purple gaze.

"What is it?" I said.

"I found your father."

I froze. I couldn't believe her words. "Is he...*alive*?"

"I don't know, dudes, he stopped breathing!" cried Twitch.

I turned to Hollywood and Twitch and back to Viorica.

She whispered, "*Your father is alive.*"

I kneeled beside Hollywood as Chuy checked his pulse. "We may be too late."

Viorica leaned, spread an elegant hand on Hollywood's chest. "He has a tiny piece of life left. I don't know if he can be saved, but we must try. I know someone on this planet that can help."

"Let's get him out of here," I said.

"I will carry them."

Bola stooped, grunted, and shoveled his hands under Twitch and Hollywood like they were babies. With the magical charm in hand, Viorica whispered some words.

The ground quaked . . . wind wailed, tossed debris into the empty gray sky. From this unsettled air emerged a bubble of silver, surface roiling and twisting with our reflections. After a few moments, it settled into the earth. Viorica waved a hand and the bubble opened.

"Follow me," she said.

And we did.

THEE END

Luis Rodriguez is a Chicago Public School teacher, scary story collector, and happily married father of two. He has several children's books published that are designed to inspire children and wake up the hero-fire in their bellies: *Clown of Aleppo*, *The Hero Inside*, and *H is for Heartbeat*. He even was crazy enough to publish a fart book, *Does Everybody Fart?* His favorite dessert is deep fried children's nightmares covered in chocolate with zombie-unicorn-blood sprinkles and a splash of pickle juice. His favorite pass time is thump wrestling Leprechaun's in abandon cemeteries. Expect more adventurous to take your heart and mind for an unforgettable ride. For updates and inspiration please follow on Instagram, Alchemy_Hero_Publishing.

10984485R00109

Made in the USA
Lexington, KY
08 October 2018